GHOSTH

POSSESS

Thomas
Walker

Titles in the Ghosthunters series

GHOSTHUNTERS

Possessed

Anthony Masters

 ORCHARD BOOKS

To Mark, Vicky and Simon
with love as always

ORCHARD BOOKS
96 Leonard Street, London EC2A 4RH
Orchard Books Australia
14 Mars Road, Lane Cove, NSW 2066
ISBN 1 86039 523 6 (hardback)
ISBN 1 86039 629 1 (paperback)
First published in hardback in Great Britain 1997
First published in paperback in Great Britain 1998
Text ©Anthony Masters 1997
1 2 3 4 5 6 02 01 00 99 98 97
The right of Anthony Masters to be identified as the
author of this work has been asserted by him in accordance
with the Copyright, Designs and Patents Act, 1988.
Printed in Great Britain
by The Guernsey Press Company Limited, Guernsey, C.I.

CHAPTER ONE

The bell rang insistently.

"Where's that coming from?" asked Jenny uneasily.

"Somewhere near Standard House," said David.

"It's a bicycle bell. I'm sure of it."

Then the sound stopped as suddenly as it had started.

The derelict quayside looked forbidding in the raw December afternoon. The sun was a cold red sponge in a slate sky and Jenny and David Golding shivered in the freezing conditions.

"What a dump," said David.

"It'll look good when Dad's finished." Jenny had enormous faith in her father. After a long struggle, the Golding family's garden centre on a wharf by the side of the Thames in the East End of London had become a success. Now Mr Golding was renting part of Standard Quay, half a mile away, to sell greenhouses and conservatories.

David wasn't so sure. He knew his father was sometimes overambitious. Standard Quay was piled high with debris, including rusting cars and trucks that had been dumped over the years. "It'll take a while to shift this lot," he said doubtfully.

"He's hired someone to do all that." Jenny was defensive. Dad had put their garden centre into profit, hadn't he? She was sure it was the most visited in East London now. He'd soon do the same for Standard Quay.

The old warehouse with its gaping windows and flaking paint loomed up above the twins. The building was four storeys high and overshadowed the quay like a fortress. Next door, dwarfed by its neighbour, was Standard House, squarely built in the nineteenth century with peeling stucco and stone columns either side of the door. Dad had told the twins that it had originally been the home of a shipwright family named Malvin but, like the warehouse, had not been occupied since the 1960s.

An abandoned church and a vicarage that was still inhabited completed the grey and rather dismal scene. In front of the warehouse was a dry dock that was also filled with discarded junk.

The ringing of the bicycle bell seemed to be coming from a small shed beside Standard House. It was commanding, urgent.

"I'd better go," David said too quickly, as if he was obeying an order.

"Wait a minute." Jenny gazed at her twin. What was the matter with him? David was always impulsive but this time he had a strange concentrated look on his face. "It's only someone messing about. Kids probably. Or someone from the vicarage." She could see a few strands of smoke rising from its chimney, seeping up into the steel grey sky. The bell was becoming increasingly strident and impatient.

"I've got to go." David was determined and Jenny felt distanced from him for the first time in a very long while. They had always been close, almost able to read one another's thoughts, and although the twins took care to have plenty of friends and not to get on each other's nerves, the closeness had always been comforting. Now David didn't seem to be around any more, despite the fact that he was still standing next to her.

The feeling was unsettling and Jenny didn't know what to do.

"Go?" she said eventually. "Go where?"

"To the bike," he replied firmly. David was gazing intently at the shed beside Standard House. "It's over there."

"That's where the ringing's coming from," Jenny agreed. "But it doesn't mean the bell's on a bike – or even that it's a bicycle bell." For some reason she felt it was important to argue, to delay him. Jenny didn't want David to go.

"What else could it be, stupid?" David's voice was rougher and coarser than usual and he began to stride through the debris towards Standard House.

"What are you playing at?" she called.

"I'm not playing at anything."

"You've altered your voice."

David broke into a run. "Why don't you push off?" he rasped.

Apprehensively, but determined not to let him out of her sight, Jenny followed.

The door of the shed was slightly open. Jenny was puzzled. She was sure it had been shut as she and David had approached.

Meanwhile, the bell continued to shrill.

David hurried into the shed before her, almost pushing her out of the way. Then she heard his cry of surprise.

"Look at this!" he yelled. "It's really cool."

His voice wasn't different any longer and Jenny immediately felt impatient with herself. Why was she so jumpy? Was it just the creepy atmosphere of the quayside?

When she reluctantly entered the dark space of the shed Jenny could just make out an old-fashioned but expensive-looking bike, in a clear plastic cover.

Then she realised the bell had stopped ringing. When did that happen? Again, like the open door, Jenny hadn't been conscious of any beginning or end. A renewed surge of anxiety made her heart thump painfully.

4

"What happened to the ringing?" she demanded.

But Jenny could see that David was hardly listening to her. Instead he was gazing at the bike fondly, as if it belonged to him.

She saw the bell under the plastic cover. Although there was no sound, it was vibrating slightly.

David flicked a switch, and by the wan light of a single bulb in the ceiling the twins could see that the bike was clamped to a workbench. It was lightweight, with low-slung handlebars, built for speed, beautifully polished so that its paint and metalwork gleamed.

"Someone's taken care of this," said Jenny.

"You bet," David breathed.

"Do you think it belongs to the vicarage?"

"Why should it?" He was immediately irritated with her.

Jenny tried to remember who lived there. Was it some relation of the boat-builder? Then she remembered Mum going on about someone she hadn't been interested in at the time.

Jenny wracked her brains and tried to remember what her mother had said. Something about "an old recluse called Gilbert Malvin . . . Used to be the local mayor . . . There's going to be a big dinner for him soon, organised by the Chamber of Commerce . . ." Then Mum had continued by telling her

Malvin had given away a fortune to the local community. It was all coming back to Jenny now and she could hear her mother's voice ringing in her ears, as sharply as the bicycle bell.

"That new sports centre would never have been built without him. You'd never imagine for one moment he was rich. An old hermit like that. They say he never comes out of the vicarage. He has a housekeeper to do for him and . . ."

"*David!* What are you doing?" Jenny cried as her twin grabbed the bike, wrenching it from the clamp and pulling off its protective cover. "You can't do that!"

"Why not?"

"It doesn't belong to you."

"Finders keepers." Jenny had never seen her brother so stubborn and pigheaded.

"Someone has been using this shed to keep this bike in. Are you crazy? It's not yours. Put it back right away." What *was* the matter with him?

"It's really light," he said, picking the bike up and then putting it down again carefully. Jumping on to the saddle, David added, "*And* beautifully made. So what if it looks a bit old-fashioned. I bet you it's fast." But he didn't look at Jenny. Not once.

"Stop this, David," she yelled at him. "It's not yours. You're stealing the bike. *Stealing* it! Can't you hear me?" Jenny had the impression that he *couldn't* hear her, that David was again in some other place, a long way away.

She felt a wave of panic as he rode towards the door. Surely it was too narrow a gap to get through, Jenny thought frantically. David was going to hurt himself badly.

But, as before, her vision seemed to have let her down, or changed in some inconceivable way, for David rode the bike through the gap – and it was wide enough to take him.

Jenny couldn't believe what she had just seen. The world, like David, seemed completely out of alignment.

Trying to recover her presence of mind, Jenny ran out after her twin, shouting at him to come back. Standing helplessly by the door of the shed, she could see David riding the bike fast along the quayside, weaving in and out of the debris. It was almost dark now and she was sure he couldn't see where he was going.

Then abruptly David switched on the headlamp, which was amazingly bright as if it had only just been fitted with new batteries. The beam picked out a rusty enamel bath filled with oily car parts, but he didn't seem to have seen it.

"David!" Jenny screamed. "Watch out!"

At the very last moment he changed course, avoiding collision, swerving past an oil drum, dodging part of a jeep and then speeding through a narrow gap between a crane and a pile of rotting crates. In a wide sweep along the very edge of the quayside, David then headed towards the deserted church of St James and the vicarage that huddled in its shadow.

Jenny tried to rationalise her thoughts. David was showing off, that was all. He did that sometimes, just to annoy her. Suddenly she lost her temper. Why on earth had she been so stupid? David was just trying to wind her up.

Jenny ran towards her twin, trying to cut him off, but as she stumbled across the chaos of the quayside she saw the vicarage door open and a tall, thin woman with her hair tied back in a bun emerged. She was accompanied by a mangy tom cat who, even in the half-light, looked unnaturally large and vicious.

"Stay there, Boris," the woman commanded and, to Jenny's surprise, the cat obeyed her as if he was a dog. "What are you doing?" the tall woman shouted as she began to stride down the vicarage steps towards David who was now cycling up to her furiously. "Get off that bike at once! That's private property that is. I'll call the police. You're one of those hooligans, aren't you? You're a thief!"

"*Shut up, Mrs Bertram!*" The voice was deeper than David's, hoarse and full of hatred. And how did he know the woman's name?

Jenny's panic returned; the rational world seemed

to have withdrawn again. She was so shocked that she couldn't speak. To her horrified amazement, she watched David ride at the woman, seeing a look of dawning alarm creep over her face in the dim porch light.

He was going to run her down.

Boris screeched and scampered back into the vicarage for shelter.

Then, just as Jenny was sure that David was going to hit Mrs Bertram, the bike reared up in a cloud of dust and he tumbled from the saddle, rolling over and over on the ground until he came to a gasping halt. The bike toppled over beside him.

Jenny came running up as David staggered to his feet, looking utterly bewildered, as if he didn't know where he was.

"I'm so sorry," she began, speaking very quickly. "My brother only borrowed the bike for a bit of fun and we'll put it back right away." She broke off as she saw Boris slowly stalk out of the vicarage again. He gazed at the bike and mewed piteously, as if he was afraid. Whilst Boris was doing this, no one spoke and Mrs Bertram, Jenny and David watched him in surprise. The tom cat padded away and then suddenly ran back inside.

Mrs Bertram dragged her eyes away from this unsettling sight. "This is monstrous," she said in a thin, steely voice. "You're just a couple of thieves."

"I don't know why I did it," said David. He was now on his feet and Jenny saw that his arm was quite badly bruised. "It came over me." He struggled for words and ran out of them. The woman stared at him in silence and then David blurted out, "I can't remember getting on or even riding the thing."

For a moment, the woman's eyes betrayed anxiety and then she returned to her angry self.

"Don't be so absurd," she snapped.

"It's true!" said David. "True as I'm standing here. I don't know what happened."

Jenny noticed that the bike's wheel was spinning slightly. She launched into what she hoped would be some kind of explanation, trying to choose her words carefully. "You see, we're the Golding twins."

"The who?"

"Mr and Mrs Golding's kids. Our parents have rented part of the warehouse and quayside."

"I'd heard." Mrs Bertram sounded disapproving. "You're selling conservatories, aren't you? From your garden centre up the road." She made it sound as if they were selling slaves. "I can't imagine who's going to come all the way down here. For conservatories." She sniffed. "But that's no excuse for aiming a stolen bike at me," she complained, but Jenny and David noticed she was calmer now.

"How did you know my name, young man?"

"Er – I just did. My dad must have told me."

Jenny was sure Dad hadn't. So how *had* David known? She remembered the other strange things that had happened, like the shifts in space she couldn't begin to explain to herself.

Mrs Bertram sniffed again. "I'm Mr Malvin's housekeeper and the bike belongs to him. Replace it exactly where you found it. Push, don't ride, and turn that headlamp off. You're wasting new batteries."

"Does a boy live in the vicarage?" asked David curiously.

Mrs Bertram gazed at him blankly. "I beg your pardon?"

Jenny noticed that Boris had returned. He gazed at the bike as if it was an unwelcome intruder.

"Does a boy –"

"Put that bike back in the shed at once. Get out of the way, Boris."

As David picked up the bike, Boris arched his back and spat, showing broken but still sharp claws. It was only then that Jenny saw the tom cat had a single yellow eye. Where the other one should have been there was an empty socket which seemed to glow darkly in the dim light.

CHAPTER TWO

Mrs Bertram watched David closely as he wheeled the bike away, followed by a still puzzled and uneasy Jenny. Her arms were folded over a green apron and Boris rubbed his nose against her long, thin legs in their thick lisle stockings.

"How *did* you know her name?" Jenny whispered to David.

"I don't know. Dad *must* have told me."

"I'm sure he didn't. And I'm sure Mum didn't either."

"So what?" he snapped. David suddenly sounded completely exhausted. Drained. "This bike's so heavy."

"What *do* you remember about all this?" demanded Jenny.

"Nothing."

"Not even riding it?" she asked in amazement.

"Not even getting on. I can only remember walking towards the door of the shed. There seemed to be a lot of light and I needed to get there fast."

"Is that all?"

He shrugged irritably. "It's nothing."

But Jenny felt very worried indeed.

"What shall we do?" asked David. There was no hint of that deeper, more rasping voice now. Perhaps she had imagined it, just like everything else.

Jenny was conscious that she kept swinging from trying to rationalise the events as they occurred – and then being swept back into being afraid again. She and David had had quite a few strange experiences and they were both careful not to let them harm their judgement, but this was different.

"Do?" Jenny said vaguely. "What do you mean?"

"Mrs Bertram could grass us up to Mum and Dad and then we'll be in dead trouble. Shall I write her a note of apology and shove it through the vicarage letterbox?" David suggested grudgingly.

"What on?"

He dug around in his pockets and found an old chocolate wrapper. "There's a pen here," he said grabbing a biro from the workbench. "What shall I say?"

Jenny took a deep breath and began to dictate a bread-and-butter letter. "'Dear Mrs Bertram, I'm sorry I took the bike and for the trouble I caused. Yours sincerely, David Golding.' There you are, keep it short and sweet."

"All right." He began to write and then howled with pain.

"What's the matter?"

"This pen's hot."

"Don't be stupid. Of course it can't be hot."

"I tell you, it's boiling hot. I can't hold the thing. It's burning my hand. Here – you try it."

Jenny took the pen only to find that it was as cold as she had expected. Was David trying to wind her up? He sometimes did, just to test her out. "Don't be a pain."

He grabbed the biro again unhappily. "You're right. That's weird. I just don't understand –"

"Get on with it!" Jenny rapped.

David began to scribble furiously and then handed her the chocolate wrapper with a disarming smile.

"'Dear Mrs Bertram,'" Jenny read. "'You're a right old misery, aren't you? I'll take the bike again any time I want – and if you try to stop me I'll ride you down.'"

Jenny looked at her brother incredulously. "Why are you being so stupid?" she snapped. "After all that's happened."

"I don't know what you mean," David said sulkily. "I've written the letter."

She tore up the note, grabbed the biro and dashed it off again on the back of an old piece of card that was on the bench. Surely David *was* only teasing her? He was never much good at choosing his moments.

"OK." She put the biro back on the workbench and then told her twin to replace the plastic on the bike. Sullenly he did as he was told and together they left the shed, walking down the cluttered quayside, back past St James's church and the vicarage.

Above them, clouds rushed across a jaundiced-looking moon, and down an alleyway, between the brooding hulk of the church and the vicarage, Jenny and David could see overgrown graves.

"I wonder what the church is like inside," Jenny said curiously.

"Overrun with rats and mice I reckon." David sounded normal enough now.

"Dad says it's going to be pulled down. No one wants to buy the place."

"I expect there's loads of bats inside as well" – David spoke with relish – "clinging to the rafters upside down."

Jenny shuddered.

"Wait." He grabbed his sister's arm as she was just about to run up the steps of the vicarage to put the note into the letterbox. "Who's that?"

They both gazed up at the window above them, seeing the pale face of an elderly man staring out across the quayside. His features were partly in shadow.

Then the curtains were hurriedly twitched back.

★

"We went to have a look at the new site," Jenny told her father over supper. She still didn't know whether Mrs Bertram was going to tell on them or not and felt it would be better to get in first to be on the safe side.

Mr Golding, however, was in a good mood. "Standard Quay's not bad, is it?" he said.

"It's a mess, Dad." David grinned at him, trying to soften the criticism.

Mrs Golding raised her eyebrows. "You don't have to tell *me*," she said. "I don't know how many skips will be needed to clear all those old vehicles."

"Don't you worry," said Mr Golding confidently. "I'm hiring Colin's truck and the council are bringing in the skips."

"Why are they being so generous?" asked Jenny.

"They're going to demolish Standard House, and the church. The decision's been made to turn the quayside into a riverside park. The old warehouse will be converted around us into industrial units eventually, so we'll have plenty of neighbours." He shot more tomato sauce on to his fish and chips.

"What about the graveyard? And the vicarage?" asked David curiously.

"The graveyard's going to become part of the park. And the vicarage is still owned by our local benefactor, Mr Malvin. Quiet bloke. Bit of a recluse, but loaded. He's putting some of his own money into the scheme."

"Have you ever met him, Dad?" asked Jenny.

"No. Can't say I have. But I will when we open up."

"Does he have a boy living there?" asked David.

There was a slight pause and Mr and Mrs Golding's eyes met for a fraction of a second.

"Not to my knowledge," Mr Golding replied stiffly. "Why do you ask?"

"We saw a bike in a shed. Bit old-fashioned but it looked as if it could really go," added David quickly.

"Can't remember any bike," muttered Mr Golding.

"It was in that shed by Standard House."

"That's nothing to do with us. Our premises are just a section at the front of the warehouse and the forecourt."

"What about the dry dock and the slipway?"

"Nothing to do with us either," he said firmly. "I expect the council will keep the slipway and fill in the dry dock. All in the fullness of time. You've been giving the place the once-over then?" Mr Golding sounded uneasy, and when Jenny glanced at her mother she looked away.

"You're sure there's no boy?" repeated David.

"Not to my knowledge. I don't think anyone lives in the vicarage but Mr Malvin and Mrs Bertram, his housekeeper. And Sarah sometimes, of course."

"Who's Sarah?"

"Mrs Bertram's little granddaughter."

"You don't want to go near that dry dock," said Mrs Golding. "Either of you. The council are going to have it properly fenced off when the site's cleared. That old tin sheeting wouldn't keep a cat out."

Jenny gave her mother a searching glance. She always knew when her parents were hiding something. "Did something happen there?" she asked gently. "You would tell us if there was anything, wouldn't you?"

There was a long silence during which Mr Golding watched his wife, clearly hoping she was going to counter the awkward question.

David waited quietly. Good old Jenny, he thought. She always gets there.

Finally, Mrs Golding cleared her throat and burst into hesitant speech. "There was a bit of a tragedy," she said unwillingly. "Way back in the sixties. A young boy got killed. He fell off his bike into that dry dock. I'm only telling you so you keep away from it. Did you hear me?" She finished in a rush, giving both the twins a threatening look.

CHAPTER THREE

Jenny woke early on Saturday morning feeling vaguely anxious, as if she had forgotten an important event. But when she wracked her brains she couldn't think what it was.

Suddenly it all came back with a nasty jolt and she remembered what had happened the night before. For a moment she felt a rush of fear, but then she decided to try and rationalise it. David had just been in a stupid mood, writing Mrs Bertram that aggressive note, and trying to wind her up at the same time. The business about the bike had been much the same; Jenny was sure David had been well in control as he rode at Mrs Bertram. He had just wanted to give her a scare.

Jenny stretched, yawned, got out of bed and glanced at her alarm clock. It was only eight on a bitterly cold morning. Through a chink in her curtains she saw heavy snow clouds in a leaden sky. She ran to the window and pulled the curtains back. Already a few flakes were drifting on to the dull grey surface of the misty River Thames that ran past her window. Below her stretched Goldings Garden Centre, straggling along the old wharf.

Then she heard the ringing sound.

Jenny realised that *this* was what she had forgotten – or more likely blocked out of her mind – when she woke this morning. How could she be so scared of a bicycle bell? But she was. Horribly scared.

The bike was leaning up against some garden furniture. Snowflakes were falling gently, softening the hard gleam of its paintwork.

Jenny couldn't seem to wrench her eyes away from it. More alarmingly, she also felt unable to move, as if she was in one of those nightmares where the dreamer is rooted to the spot. She could sense power, a force pinning her feet to the bedroom carpet, her eyes on the bike. Despite the snow, the polished steel of the handlebars glinted at her, the shine locked into her eyes.

Jenny was conscious of not blinking, holding her breath, her heart pounding to a painful rhythm, the ringing sound controlling her. Then the bell croaked like a frog and she was released.

Shivering, Jenny opened the door and ran down the passage.

When she burst into David's bedroom, he was asleep, in his usual position on his side. Jenny bent over him protectively, not really knowing why she was doing so, but his breathing was deep, regular and normal.

She couldn't hear the bicycle bell from here and wondered if it had stopped ringing. Then, watching her twin closely, Jenny noticed he had suddenly started to grip the duvet with his right hand. His lips began to form silent words but she couldn't make out what he was saying.

"Go away, Bud," said David, still deep in sleep. "I don't want you."

But the more he tried to order him away, the more tightly Bud closed in. Their spirits fused as the bike skimmed over thick snow.

"Wake up, David." Jenny grabbed at his arm, but he suddenly lashed out at her. Had she not dodged out of the way she would have caught the blow full in the face. "David. What are you doing?" He had never hit her before. Why now?

He woke, gazing up at her, his forehead covered in shiny sweat.

"What's the matter?" he asked blearily.

"You tried to hit me."

He shook his head, unable to believe what she was saying.

"And the bike's outside."

"*What?*" He sat up immediately, the sweat intensifying. "The what?"

"You heard. The bike."

There was a long pause while David stared at her.

His eyes were blinking rapidly and he gripped the duvet so hard that his knuckles whitened.

"You were saying something in your sleep. But I couldn't make out what it was."

David didn't reply for a long time and then he ignored her question. "Where's the bike?" he finally muttered.

"Leaning against a garden seat."

"How did it get there?"

"You must have taken it again. You're going to be in dead trouble."

"I *didn't* take it."

"How else would it have got there?" Jenny was getting heated, more out of anxiety than anger.

"I *didn't* take it!" he repeated angrily, tears in his eyes.

"OK." David was so upset that she gave in. Why was he acting so much out of character? Could her brother be ill? Running a fever?

"We've got to get the bike back to Mrs Bertram," she told him.

"I'm not riding it," David snapped. "No chance."

"I think you should." Jenny was doubtful.

"I'm not riding that bike!" he yelled. "Someone's messing about. That boy at the vicarage. He must have ridden the bike over here."

"There *isn't* a boy at the vicarage."

"Then who rode it? That old bat Bertram? Or

Gilbert Malvin? They're trying to get me into trouble." David sounded as if he was about seven years old. "I'm going fishing. I'm not having anything more to do with that bike. If you want to take it back, then it's up to you."

"OK," said Jenny. "Just leave it to me."

"Be careful," he muttered.

CHAPTER FOUR

Jenny hurried downstairs feeling anxious, not wanting to touch the bike either. As she walked out of the kitchen and into the old conservatory where they kept their outside shoes, she gazed down at David's trainers and a cold feeling spread in her stomach. They were covered in mud and she knew they hadn't been in that state when they had both got home last night. David must have gone out again and taken the bike. So why wasn't he admitting it? What on earth was going on?

The snow was falling more heavily now and Jenny had the curious and unsettling feeling of being surrounded, of being watched.

Her parents were having a Saturday morning lie-in, so at least they wouldn't be asking any questions. Not yet, anyway.

Then she heard the slightest of sounds. Jenny turned round abruptly to see David standing by the door, silently watching her with an unfamiliar look in his eyes. He was very still.

"I'm going fishing now," he said. His voice was strained, determined, as if he had fought to make the decision against heavy opposition.

"Don't you want any breakfast?" she asked hesitantly.

"I've got to go."

"You sure you didn't fetch the bike?" Jenny tried one more time, deliberately sounding as uncritical as possible.

"Why should I want the thing?" His voice was childishly stubborn and she gazed at him, startled. The look had gone from his eyes, but now he seemed as afraid as she was. "Why should I want the bike?" David repeated shakily. "I've got a perfectly good one of my own. With a load more gears. That thing's old-fashioned and useless."

"I just wish I knew how it got there," was all Jenny could find to say, still trying to ignore the muddy trainers.

David set off for his fishing trip, grabbing some bread and cheese and pedalling away on his own bike. Jenny got a shock when she heard a bell ringing, but then she realised it was David's, which made a much clearer, more mellow sound.

After breakfast, and with her parents still asleep, she went outside to find the snow had stopped falling. It was deadly cold and she was sure her brother wouldn't last long at the old reservoir a few miles up the road. Already her own hands were beginning to feel frozen and Jenny dashed back inside to grab a pair of warm fur-lined gloves.

When she came out again, she glanced up at the sky to see more snow clouds gathering. She began to worry about David again. Why had he insisted on going fishing today of all days? He hadn't been for ages. In fact, she had thought he had given up what had once been an obsessive hobby.

It was almost as if he had wanted to get away, to put distance between himself and the old bike.

Jenny walked over and touched the handlebars. They were very cold. Then she swung a leg over and got on to the saddle which was just the right size for her. To ride the bike seemed the most natural thing in the world. Besides, she knew she had to.

Jenny began to pedal her way round the narrow paths of the garden centre. She rode slowly, knowing the surface below her was snow-bound and icy, anxious to keep the heavy bike stable.

Heavy? Suddenly it wasn't heavy at all. The bike was *light*. Then the bell began to ring and she gazed down in amazement. Her hand was nowhere near it. The wheels of the bike were turning fast, and when she tried to take her feet off the pedals she found she couldn't; it was as if they were stuck with superglue. She knew she had lost all control. The bike was in charge.

She began to circle the garden centre, speeding up, screaming in terror, sure that she would crash at any moment, go spinning into a cold frame, or the empty display swimming pool or, worse still, the river itself.

Desperately, Jenny tried to steer but the bike had a will of its own, and although she fought to turn the handlebars they were rigid, set on their own course. Now she knew what David had been so afraid of. Now she knew why he had gone fishing. The bike had been waiting for one of them.

Again the speed increased until everything became a blur. The air about her was freezing as the bike headed for a row of brightly coloured garden gnomes, turning at the last moment to set a new course over the thick snow on the path through the herb garden. At the bottom was a wall. She screamed again as the bike showed no sign of stopping.

Then, at the very last moment, the brakes were slammed on. The bike reared up like a horse, turned on one wheel and sped back the way it had come.

"You're going too fast!" yelled a familiar voice and Jenny saw David's blurred face. He'd come back. He hadn't deserted her after all.

"I can't stop!" she shouted desperately. "It won't let me."

David didn't hesitate. With his rod still lashed to his crossbar he pedalled as fast as he could towards her, skidding on the snow but somehow managing to remain upright. David sped on but he stood no chance of catching her up.

"It's going to crash," she wailed, seeing the bike was now heading for a display of garden ponds and fountains. Then she heard a squeal and realised the bike was jamming on its own brakes again.

The pedals released her and Jenny found herself flying over the handlebars towards the compost heap. She hit the filthy, foul-smelling mulch at considerable speed.

David was only a couple of metres behind as the bike slowly toppled over on its side, bell ringing and wheels spinning. Then suddenly it was still and silent.

Jenny wasn't hurt. But as she struggled out of the compost she knew she could have been badly injured and felt light-headed with a mixture of shock and relief.

"You came back," she gasped.

"I had to," replied David miserably. "I was a coward to run away."

Jenny eyed the silent bike. "What's happening?" she pleaded. "You know something, don't you?"

"I dreamt about this boy," said David abruptly. "He was about our age. I think his name was Bud. But I'm not sure. I think the bike belongs to him."

"Where is he then?" Jenny gazed at her twin

hopelessly. The feeling of everything running out of control was back.

"He's dead."

"How do you make that out?" Jenny spoke slowly, not wanting to alarm David, panic spreading inside her.

"Maybe he's the boy Mum said got killed in the sixties. The one who fell off his bike into the dry dock."

"And someone repaired it afterwards? And kept it beautiful? In memory of him?" Jenny's words were tumbling over each other now.

"Could be," replied David. "I don't like any of this. He – this Bud – it's as if he's taking me over."

Jenny shivered. "It's all a mistake," she said feebly, but her twin wasn't listening.

"I think he can get inside me, specially when I'm on the bike. That's why I wanted to go fishing."

"David. You've got to tell me. Did you collect the bike from Standard Quay last night?"

"I don't know. That's the awful thing," he replied, looking increasingly afraid.

"When I'm on the bike, I don't remember any-thing about *me*. Do you see what I mean? Those trainers of mine were really muddy and they weren't last night." He paused. "Were they?"

"No," Jenny replied miserably. "They weren't."

★

"What are we going to do?" David asked fearfully. He looked dependently at his sister as if she could solve the problem for him.

"We've got to keep calm," said Jenny. "We've got to reason it all out. Why should this Bud pick on you?"

"You *know* why. It's happened before. We're psychic, I guess. Bud's using us. Using me."

"We've got to take the bike back to Standard House," said Jenny.

"It's got a will of its own," said David. He had a look of real terror on his face. "Bud's will. I'll get taken over again."

Jenny could hardly bear to think about the possibility. Bud seemed to have so much anger in him if her recent bike ride had been anything to go by. It seemed he was playing with them both at the moment. But did he have a use for them later? "It's beginning to snow again," she said quietly. "We've *got* to get that bike back."

"I'll push it," said David, working up the courage that she always so much admired in him. "Surely nothing can happen if I just push."

"It's too dangerous. *I'll* do the pushing."

"It's OK –" David began. "He's a threat to us both. You could have been hurt badly rather than just being dumped in a compost heap."

The bell started ringing again and the bike came

slowly upright.

"I don't believe that," muttered David.

"You have to," Jenny snapped. "It's happening."

For a moment the bike remained stationary. Then they both heard a low chuckle. It was an incredibly sinister sound and seemed to vibrate menacingly inside the twins' heads for some time.

Without warning, the bike began to pedal itself away down the quayside in the direction of Standard House. Its bell rang cheerfully, almost cheekily, as the snow began to fall once more.

CHAPTER FIVE

"I've never seen anything like it," said a bemused David as they walked back to the house. "The bike rode itself away. What would happen if anyone else saw it?"

"That's the point," said Jenny. She was just as shocked. "They won't. Not unless they've got the sight."

"You mean they just wouldn't see the thing?" demanded David incredulously.

"I'm sure they wouldn't," she insisted. Jenny was quiet for a while. Then she muttered, almost to herself, "What does this Bud want?"

"He wants me," snapped David. "*I'm* his victim."

Jenny wasn't so sure.

Then David grinned weakly. "Maybe no one will see the riderless bike, but they might have another shock coming."

Jenny gazed at her twin in bewilderment. "What do you mean?" she asked suspiciously.

"You," David replied triumphantly. "The compost monster!"

★

"What's that smell?" asked Mr Golding. He was standing outside the bathroom in his dressing gown as Jenny emerged with her dirty clothes. Dad didn't exactly look in a good mood.

"What have you two been up to? Messing about like little kids. I'd have thought you were too grown up for all that. I suppose David pushed you into the compost, did he? You know, I don't think that boy's ever going to – "

"It's snowing, Dad." She tried to divert him. "It's getting quite thick." Then Jenny realised that she had said absolutely the wrong thing.

"That's just what's worrying me," he began anxiously. "I was only saying to your mother that we'll never make the start we need to at Standard Quay with all this bad weather. But you haven't answered my question. How did you – "

"I fell off my bike," she replied too quickly. "It wasn't David's fault. He wasn't anywhere near me."

"All right." Mr Golding wasn't really listening now.

"What's the matter?" asked Jenny. "The *real* matter?" She knew him of old. Her father was rather like David. Spontaneous. They didn't stop to think things out. They saw opportunities, and went for them and got upset afterwards.

"Nothing," came the predictable reply.

"I'm sure the conservatories are a good idea.

Everything else has sold well. Why shouldn't they?"

"The garden centre took a long time to get going," he began in a voice of doom.

"But we *got* going, didn't we? That's the main thing. Now we're expanding."

"And then there's that vicarage. The place fair gives me the creeps."

"Why?" Jenny asked sharply.

"Dunno. Maybe it's Mrs Bertram. Every time I go over there she keeps watching me. And when she's not watching, her boss is. Malvin gives me the creeps too. Sits upstairs in that room of his and stares out all the time. Why does he do it?"

Jenny didn't know. "Wait till the punters are coming in. They'll give the place a bit of life, won't they?"

"It'll just give old Malvin more to watch," Mr Golding said pessimistically. "*And* complain about."

David had intended to play football that afternoon and Jenny had planned to go ice-skating with her friend Tracy. But because of the snow, they stayed at home, watching TV and mildly bickering.

Jenny felt as restless as her twin. All she could think about was the ghost bike (as she now thought of it), and its owner – Bud – if that really was his name. She knew David was feeling the same.

But he was in a much worse position than she

was. Bud could make David do things that he couldn't remember. Then there was the weird business of the bike pedalling off on its own. She had tried to talk to David about it several times, but he didn't seem to want to discuss the situation. Was he trying to blot it all out of his mind?

After lunch, she found David lying on his bed, staring up at the ceiling, his eyes wide open and his fists clenched hard.

"What are you doing?" she asked tentatively.

"Don't I get any privacy?" he complained. "I bet other boys' sisters don't keep coming into their rooms – even if they are twins." He frowned at her resentfully.

"I'm worried about you."

"I'm fine," he said, just like his father.

"What are you doing?" she persisted.

"Nothing." As he spoke, David suddenly broke down, burying his face in the pillow. "*You* don't have to keep him out, do you?" His voice was muffled and shaky. "He's been telling me to do things. Ever since lunch."

"What things?" Jenny asked, her heart beginning to pound.

"To ride the bike. I don't want to. You've got to tell him to go away." David turned over and gazed up at her. She could detect the raw fear in him and the inability to cope on his own. There *must* be something she could do, thought Jenny, some way she could fight Bud too. But how? Suddenly a different look came into her twin's eyes. A sort of glint.

David was still staring at her but he was no longer appealing for help. Instead he was hostile and threatening. Jenny could also smell something. Was it earth?

"*Get out of our room*," he said in a voice that was startlingly different from his own, husky and arrogant.

"Whose room?" she asked, trying to keep her nerve and failing.

"*We don't want you in here*." David's eyes were like little coals of angry fire and his fists were doubled up aggressively. He wasn't fighting Bud any longer. Bud had won. Bud was inside him.

"Leave my brother alone," Jenny snarled. Her temper rose and with it a greater determination.

David grinned, but in a way she had never seen before. It was her twin's face but not his expression, which was mocking and darkly angry. Then the look went as if a switch had suddenly been turned off.

Jenny relaxed slightly.

"What's happening?" asked David miserably. "I can't remember. Was he inside me?"

She couldn't bring herself to answer him.

"*Was* he there?" David repeated.

Biting her lip, Jenny nodded.

He immediately looked defeated. "I tried to fight him," he whispered. "I really tried. I used all my willpower but he was too strong."

"You've got to fight harder," she said. "I'll help."

"What good could that do? It's me he wants. Not you."

Jenny and David gazed at each other hopelessly, the fear hardening inside them like great blocks of ice.

"I'm so tired," he said. "I want to sleep."

"I don't think you should do that."

"In case he comes again? There's nothing I can do if he does." He sounded completely apathetic. "He can come in at any time and use me in any way he likes."

"You've *got* to fight," Jenny shouted at him.

David simply turned over in bed and buried his face in his pillow again.

What was she going to do? she wondered desperately. Who was this boy? This aggressive spirit? What did he want with them?

Never had she been so afraid before. In the past, she and David had been a unit. Now they were split down the middle. Despite the central heating, the room was freezing cold, but while Jenny shivered she could see that David was still sweating profusely.

Jenny stayed on guard by her brother's bedside for the next half-hour. When he seemed to be sleeping peacefully Jenny slipped back to her own bedroom, to gaze out at the blanket of falling snow. It had covered the wharf quite deeply now. Ice crackled on the sides of the Thames as, dark and silent, it hurtled past on a vicious tide. The world around her that had once been so familiar now seemed alien, Bud's presence brooding over it all, commanding and malicious.

Jenny knew she couldn't watch her brother all the time. But what would happen if she didn't?

"Penny for them."

She started. Jenny had left her door half open to listen for anything that might happen to David. Now Mum was standing on the threshold.

"I'm just watching the snow."

"Feeling trapped? That's the way it makes me feel. And of course your father's concerned about Standard Quay opening late. Regular worry-guts he is." Mum cleared her throat. "And what's up with you and David?"

"Nothing," said Jenny miserably.

Mum looked at her watch, knowing that her daughter was in no mood to talk to her now. "Snow or no snow, I've got to nip down the road and see how Mrs Rogers is. Can't have her getting cold in this lot." Mrs Rogers was an old-age pensioner who Mrs Golding kept a relentless eye on. "Your dad's down in the office, looking over the new plans. He'll be there for hours, but I won't be long."

"OK."

"Sure you're all right?" Like Jenny, her mother could easily detect uneasy feelings; very little escaped her.

She tried to reply casually. "I get that trapped feeling too, Mum. But the clouds aren't so heavy now. Maybe the snow's going to stop."

After her mother had left, the weather cleared slightly and wan sunlight began to filter through.

Now the blanketing feeling had gone, Jenny felt easier in her mind. Maybe she was getting all this out of proportion. In the past she and David had always managed to cope. All they had to do was to work together, to try and share each other's thoughts more. They needed to work out a plan.

Jenny hurried back to her twin's room, only to find him sleeping deeply and peacefully. He was no longer sweating and seemed to be much more relaxed. The plan will keep, she told herself. He'll definitely wake up for tea and afterwards we'll talk.

Jenny returned to her own room, picked up a book and lay on her bed. She tried to read, but almost immediately she had an overpowering urge to sleep. Her eyelids grew so heavy that the book slipped out of her fingers and fell on to the floor.

Just as Jenny drifted off, she thought she heard a mocking laugh, but she was too far gone to stay awake.

CHAPTER SIX

David knew that he had to get up. He had to do as he was told. He had to go to Standard Quay. David tried to fight but Bud had swept in on a tide of sleep, taking him over at once. The tide was like a wave of molten lead that filled the caves of his mind with Bud's will. David was swamped. He had no energy of his own.

He went downstairs, and without even bothering to check if anyone was around David opened the back door and walked out into the freezing cold.

Jenny woke, once again sure there was something wrong but not knowing what it was. She lay in bed for a moment, surprised she had slept in the afternoon. She had never done this before. Why today? Hazily, she began to remember the events of this morning. Had they really exhausted her so much?

She got up stiffly, her head muzzy, and went over to the window. The snow had stopped falling but it was thick on the ground and virtually undisturbed – except for the trail of footprints.

Jenny gazed at them in horror. She was sure they were David's.

She couldn't risk going to find her parents. Jenny knew she had to get after David. Fast.

Her feet seemed to fly over the deep snow, and she began to get the strange feeling that she was being pulled along by a relentless force. When she looked down, however, Jenny could see that her feet were making deep imprints in the snow. So why wasn't she feeling the strain?

Gradually the sensation of being propelled increased and with it renewed alarm. She tried to stop, to resist the force, but she couldn't. Jenny had to keep going. Did Bud want her too? Was she now obeying a summons?

When she arrived at Standard Quay the feeling of propulsion drained away, leaving her exhausted.

David was nowhere to be seen and Jenny's leg muscles ached. Had she actually forced herself along? Had the propulsion been her own? But she was too concerned for her twin to give the problem any more thought. Where was he?

The brooding warehouse was stark against the snow-laden sky, and Standard House, St James's church and the vicarage seemed like a forbidden city. The quayside also looked smaller, boxed in, almost as if the buildings had silently inched forward.

Jenny could see a number of different footprints in the snow. Then she felt a cold, prickling sensation down her back. She was sure she was being watched.

Slowly Jenny turned to gaze into the windows of the vicarage. A curtain was abruptly pulled back on the ground floor, while at a first-floor window she saw the pale face she and David had noticed yesterday. Was this Gilbert Malvin, the elderly recluse?

Jenny stared back but the face didn't withdraw and continued to watch her inscrutably.

Boris the tom cat slowly emerged from the passage between the church and the vicarage that led to the graveyard. He gazed up at her, arching his back, his empty eye socket as chilling as ever. Then he padded away across the snow to Standard House as twilight crept along the quayside.

Then Jenny saw a wan light in the shed.

Despite the fact that she had felt so compelled to come, she now had to force herself to walk across the snow. The only other illumination came from the vicarage windows, but they seemed just as pale and gloomy as the light in the shed.

Suddenly a snowball caught Jenny squarely between the shoulderblades.

She turned round with a grunt of pain to see a little

girl with fair hair and a round face. She had podgy cheeks, a snub nose and blue eyes.

For a second the girl glared at Jenny and then she ran away, her coat flying out behind her. She pushed open the door to the vicarage and then slammed it hard. The noise was like a muffled gunshot on the snowbound quayside and it seemed to echo off the stone face of Standard House.

Why did she do that? Jenny wondered. She felt hurt, more mentally than physically, and tears pricked at the back of her eyes. Why was everything turning out so badly? Wasn't it enough for her brother to be possessed?

She glanced up at Standard House. One of the upstairs windows was open, but there was no one there that she could see.

"David?" she called. "Are you up there, David?"

There was no reply and a windless, deadening silence seemed to coil around her suffocatingly as she saw the front door was also slightly open. Why hadn't she noticed that before? Jenny felt confused and slightly sick. Then the drawing sensation powerfully gripped her again and she found herself walking towards the house.

Slowly, Jenny climbed the steep flight of steps to the front door. Now she could see into a pitch-black interior that smelt of mould and damp and something else she couldn't identify for a moment. Then she realised it was earth. Hadn't she smelt that somewhere before?

As she stood on the threshold, more snow began to fall, the white blanket quickly obliterating the footprints across the quayside. There was no trace of her now. No trace of anyone.

Suddenly the bicycle bell began to ring, softly at first and then building up into its usual shrill clamour.

The sound broke the spell and Jenny realised, with tremendous relief, that she no longer had to enter Standard House. She had her own free will again.

Jenny ran down the steps towards the shed and the noise, the snowflakes settling on her quickly. She turned back for a moment to see that her footsteps were covered yet again. Now she felt as if she hardly existed.

"David –" Jenny dragged open the door, only to find the bike lying on the floor, wrenched from its protective covering, a wheel spinning, the bell still shrilling.

But there was no sign of her twin.

Was that another door at the back of the shed? she wondered. It was thickly covered in a tangle of cobwebs.

Then Jenny heard shouting.

The words were impossible to make out but she

knew they were angry and threatening. Jenny shivered, suddenly feeling that something very bad was about to happen.

Trembling, she felt her gaze riveted to the cobwebs, which at first looked like fragile mist. Then they bulged, stretched and straightened and a faint human form came hurtling towards her.

The shouting continued in the blurred distance as the figure took a firmer shape.

The boy was dark, lean and frightened-looking. He brushed past Jenny, and his touch made a cold ache in her head as if she was having a terrible bout of toothache. Then he was gone, and with him the all-pervading chill. But lingering on was the smell, that same smell she had detected in Standard House. A smell of earth. Raw and rooty. The smell of the grave.

A little wind seemed to come from nowhere – just like the boy. Snow flurried in through the door, the bicycle wheel turned faster, and something blew down from a shelf on to the workbench.

Jenny found she was gazing at a crumpled, torn book which was covered in dust.

Hesitantly, she picked it up and saw that it was a copy of *Eagle Annual 1962*. Even without the mildew and decay the book looked well thumbed and battered.

She turned the pages, gasping as a couple of

earwigs ran out from the spine. Then, on the title page, Jenny saw the inscription:

For my dear godson, Bud.
Your affectionate Uncle Gilbert

"David!" she called, wanting to hear her own voice, to grasp at normality. "Are you hiding? Where are you?"

Suddenly the window of the shed opened and closed, sending up a cloud of dust. As Jenny began to choke, she heard the sound of chuckling.

"Stop winding me up, Dave," she yelled, but she knew for an absolute certainty that the chuckling was nothing like her brother's laughter.

Jenny glanced at the window. Some of the grime had been shaken free but now the glass was misting over. Then she saw words beginning to form in the condensation, scrawled in finger writing:

BUD'S HERE

As she watched, the message faded and she could hardly believe that it had ever been there in the first place. The wheel of the bike had stopped spinning, the bell had stopped ringing, the shed was dead. Bud's dead too, she thought. Yet to her, and particularly to David, he was still very much alive.

Then Jenny saw the door was slowly opening and the scream seemed to stick in her throat. For a moment she had the terrible feeling that she was going to suffocate. Then David stood in the doorway and she breathed a long sigh of relief.

"I was looking for you," he said.

"I was looking for *you*," Jenny snapped, angry now. "Why did you go off without me? And where have you been?"

"I don't know. I felt I had to come here."

"So did I," Jenny admitted, her voice shaking, and she told David about what had happened.

He only half listened to her, as if he was still partly elsewhere. Why was her twin shutting her out again? Jenny fought for control, knowing that if she showed him how afraid she was, Bud would win.

"What does he want?" she asked David gently.

"I don't know."

"Doesn't he say?"

"He doesn't *say* anything." David sighed and Jenny realised that he was with her again.

"I only wish he would. I just blank out and he's there in my place. At least, I think that's the way it happens."

"He died violently," Jenny said. "Could that have something to do with it?"

David shrugged hopelessly.

"There must be a reason for his spirit hanging around."

"I think it's more than that." He was shivering. "Much more."

"What?"

"He makes me do terrible things. Like ride the bike at Mrs Bertram. Do you think he wants to kill her?"

"Of course not," said Jenny, too quickly and unconvincingly. Then she tried to change the subject. "There was a girl outside. She chucked a snowball at me and then ran back into the vicarage. She was only young. Eight, maybe," said Jenny, adding gloomily, "She looked as if she really hated me."

"I'm sure Mrs Bertram and this Gilbert Malvin know more than we do," David said eagerly. "Can't we go and see them? Find out what they know?"

"We aren't exactly top favourites."

"She protects him," said David unexpectedly.

"What?" There was a change in his voice that was becoming all too familiar. "What did you say?" Jenny repeated.

"*He made my father run away. He made me die.*" Bud was back, harsh and threatening. "*I hate Uncle Gilbert.*"

CHAPTER SEVEN

David picked up the bike, looking away from Jenny, staring down.

"Don't get on it!" she yelled but her twin ignored her, and when Jenny tried to grab him he pushed her away with such force that she fell against a steel tool cupboard with a resounding crash. "You hurt me," she whimpered, but he didn't take the slightest notice.

Instead, he jumped on the saddle.

"Where are you going?"

But David was already cycling out of the shed and into the snow.

Jenny ran to the door, her heart pounding and with a terrible ache in the pit of her stomach.

"David!" She screamed his name over and over again. "David. You've got to stop." Then, in desperation, she yelled, "Bud! Give him back. Please!"

Mrs Bertram was coming out of the open door of the vicarage while the little girl who had thrown the snowball hovered on the step.

"Get off that bike!" Jenny screamed at David.

Mrs Bertram seemed rooted to the spot, watching the bike race towards her as the snow flurried around its wheels.

"David," yelled Jenny. "Stop!" Then she had an idea. "Fight him, David. Fight him with your will. Say no to Bud. Say no to him."

"Who?" Mrs Bertram looked dazed. "*Who* did you say?"

But Jenny didn't have a chance to reply as David jammed on the brakes of the ghost bike which skidded in a huge arc, powdered snow swirling about him.

Then, as if in slow motion, he and the bike keeled over, just half a metre from Mrs Bertram's Wellington boots.

The little girl ran down the steps towards them and stood beside her grandmother protectively.

"What name did you say?" she asked Jenny accusingly.

"Bud," Jenny replied.

"Is that a joke? A cruel joke?"

"No." Jenny wracked her brains for an answer. "I saw his name in a book – in the shed. It was . . ."

"The bike belonged to Bud Malvin," said Mrs Bertram coolly. All her indignation seemed to have been swept away and she looked numb and stricken. "Bud was my employer's nephew and godson." She paused and then hurried on. "Bud was killed when he fell off that bike into the dry dock thirty years ago. So – when you said his name you can imagine it came as something of a shock."

But all Jenny could think about was David. He'd beaten Bud. Fought and beaten him. But she knew he would have to strengthen his willpower much more if he was to continue to hold him off.

What does she know? Jenny wondered as she gazed up at Mrs Bertram's pinched and haggard face. Does she know Bud's spirit's on the loose? Has she guessed that he's reached us? Then she tried to calm herself. Mrs Bertram probably had no idea of what was going on and it was just Bud's name that had shaken her up so badly.

"I'm telling you all this now, so you'll understand and leave the bike alone. I'm going to have it moved back to the vicarage." Mrs Bertram reached for her granddaughter's hand, as if she desperately needed comfort.

"Tell us some more about Bud. Did he live here?" asked David, suddenly back to his normal self.

Mrs Bertram nodded reluctantly. "I have to tell you that Bud's father was a bad lot and it was his fault that his son was killed. He'd been involved in a robbery . . ." Suddenly her voice was high with emotion and both David and Jenny wondered if she was going to cry. In the end, however, Mrs Bertram controlled herself. "Gilbert was devoted to

Bud." She paused and swallowed. "And still is. Why do you think the bike's in such good repair, despite the fact that it's over thirty years old?" She looked at it distastefully. "I hate the thing."

"Because it belonged to Bud?" asked Jenny. "I mean, because he was killed on it?"

"It's not just that," Mrs Bertram said. "This is my granddaughter, Sarah. She's staying with me for a week. She's tried to ride that bike and it hurt her. I don't know why you children don't listen to me. She had no right to touch it either."

"*Hurt* her?" demanded David. "What do you mean?"

Sarah started to say something but her grandmother quickly interrupted.

"She tried to push it out of the shed the other day and she got a nasty cut. She came back to me, crying her eyes out."

Jenny and David gave Sarah a curious glance and she looked away. Had Bud managed to reach her too?

"You make it sound as if the bike has a life of its own," said David carefully.

Mrs Bertram gave him a suspicious glance. "It's too big for her, that's all. I've warned Sarah to keep away from it and now I'm warning you. For different reasons, of course." She gave them a sharp glance, but Jenny thought it was a pleading one as well. "Please don't touch it. If we're all going to be neighbours in the future, let's try and understand and respect each other. The reason Mr Malvin hasn't moved the bike is that Bud apparently used that shed a lot. He loved to tinker with it there."

"Did you know Bud?" asked David curiously.

"No. I've only been in Mr Malvin's employ for the last ten years. But I know about his grief, of course. I don't think it'll ever stop."

Then Sarah said quietly, her eyes on her grandmother, "He's happier now though."

"What do you mean?" asked Jenny, but Mrs Bertram turned on Sarah angrily.

"What did I say about – "

"Mr Malvin's not so miserable now. He's fallen in love with my gran."

"Sarah!"

"They might even get married."

"Be quiet, Sarah. How dare you talk such nonsense to two perfect strangers."

David thought Mrs Bertram was blushing and Jenny was sure of it. There was something rather touching about her obvious embarrassment.

"I must be getting in." She grabbed Sarah's hand.

Then the bell began to ring. But ringing didn't really describe the appalling sound. It was as if someone was grinding their teeth.

David turned away, clenching his fists, as if the shrilling was making his nerves scream, like someone writing on a blackboard with a piece of squeaky chalk.

Bewildered by David's tortured expression, dragging Sarah with her, Mrs Bertram fled inside and slammed the door.

CHAPTER EIGHT

"Don't touch," warned Jenny as David bent down to stand the bike upright.

"We can't leave it out in the snow."

"Yes we can." She grabbed his arm, knowing that if Bud was around she might get hurt.

But David simply backed off, muttering, "Maybe you're right."

"I *am* right. Mrs Bertram will put it away."

"Would she dare?"

"Of course." Jenny was confident. "Anyone who can't be reached by Bud can handle the bike and do what they like with it."

"That's everyone except us."

"And Sarah."

"You mean Bud can reach her too?"

"I think so."

"I get the idea," began David slowly, "that he doesn't exactly like Sarah."

"He doesn't seem to *like* us much," Jenny reminded her twin.

"So why's he trying to take me over?" asked David bitterly. "How can I get rid of him?"

"Use your willpower. It's just worked, hasn't it?

So it's got to work again."

"Suppose it's a never-ending battle," said David gloomily. "Suppose I have to fight Bud every day of my life?"

As they started to walk back home, the twins heard a hissing sound and saw Sarah standing halfway up the passage between the church and the vicarage that led to the graveyard. She had a finger pressed to her lips and was signalling them to join her.

Hoping the ever alert Mrs Bertram wasn't going to spring out on them yet again, they edged forward.

"What do you want?" asked Jenny disapprovingly. She hadn't forgotten the snowball.

"I thought you were an enemy," Sarah whispered. "But now I'm not so sure." She paused. "You've seen him too, then?"

"Who?" demanded David impatiently.

"The boy, of course. The boy in the shed. I've seen him, lots of times – and not just there." Sarah seemed to be full of a rising excitement mixed with anxiety.

"Where else?" asked Jenny, more encouragingly.

"In Standard House. Watching from the window."

"Have you ever been inside?"

Sarah shuddered. "I'd never go in. It's dark and shut up and bad things happened there."

"What sort of things?" asked David, trying to draw her out.

"Things," she muttered defiantly.

Is she trying to find out what we know while we're trying to find out what *she* knows? wondered Jenny.

"Have you see him or not?" demanded Sarah.

Jenny took the plunge, but was careful to sound vague. "We think so."

"Why can *we* see him, when no one else can?" asked Sarah.

"I don't know," said Jenny.

"Have you ever seen a ghost before?" asked David abruptly.

"I'm not sure. Maybe. Sometimes I can see people in shadowy places. Do you know what I mean?" Sarah glanced up at Jenny appealingly. "This boy," she continued. "He's dangerous. He wants to hurt people."

"Do you know why?" asked David urgently.

Sarah shook her head and then looked at them speculatively. "He wants to pay someone out."

"Like your gran? But why?"

"*I* don't know." She brushed past them, suddenly looking as frightened of the twins as she was of the boy.

Why are we all playing games? wondered Jenny. Why can't we tell the truth? But then Sarah was very young and obviously frightened. She probably didn't know the truth anyway.

"I've got to go in for tea. Gran will be furious if she finds I've gone out again." Sarah ran back down the passage and then paused. "He's buried, you know, that boy. He's buried in the graveyard. One day I watched him go home."

"Home?" asked Jenny curiously.

"It's all overgrown down there. That's why he's cross with me – because I saw him. He's not right, this boy."

"I know he's not."

Sarah ran on down the passage and disappeared, presumably into the back door of the vicarage.

"It must be awful to be left alone like that," muttered David.

They both looked down towards the graveyard.

"It's so cold there," said Jenny, her voice breaking. "So cold."

"Bud's dangerous," David reminded her. "It's not fair. He can't live in me, like I'm his house or something."

"We'll fight him together," Jenny promised, knowing how inadequate she sounded.

"He can make me do what he wants."

"You've got to use your willpower," Jenny repeated. "You've always had so much of it. You know it can work now."

"I know when he's coming," muttered David. "There's a sort of cloud in my head, like fog. Like snow."

"So that's the warning then. You've got *time* to fight him. I can feel him too, only not nearly so much. I suppose he picked on you because you're a boy – because he can be part of you much easier."

"I wish he'd been a girl," replied David savagely. "Then you could have had a taste of it."

"I'd like to take him on," said Jenny fiercely.

"No." He was suddenly more resolute. "He's my fight. Not yours."

"There's Boris." Jenny watched the cat slink down the passage. "You don't reckon he could be aware of Bud's presence too, do you?"

David laughed derisively. Then he glanced at the cat's empty eye socket and stopped.

CHAPTER NINE

Jenny and David slept deeply that night.

David had spent a frantic hour trying to stay awake, afraid to let go in case Bud slipped into his mind. The fact that he had actually succeeded in breaking Bud's all-consuming will by forcing the bike to the ground did not bring him much comfort. David knew what an enormous effort it had been. Would he be capable of putting up that kind of mental struggle again?

Eventually he had drifted into merciful oblivion.

Jenny had every intention of spending the night checking on her twin, getting up every hour on the hour, but she was so exhausted that she slept almost immediately.

No more snow fell but it was deadly cold and the ice on the banks of the Thames grew wider. The freeze had London in its grip and the forecasters said it was going to continue.

When Jenny woke she jumped out of bed and hurried into David's room, guilty at having slept so well, fearful that Bud might have made her twin get up yet again, only to find the ghost bike waiting for him outside. How could she have been so selfish? She should have watched over him. Her panic rose as she opened David's door.

He *looked* peaceful enough and Jenny didn't know whether to wake him or not. Eventually, she touched his shoulder and then shook it gently. Slowly, David surfaced.

"What do you want?"

"To make sure you're OK."

"Of course I am." He sounded almost angry, as if he didn't want to wake to such a threatening and unpredictable world.

"I was worried."

"About Bud? So am I." He sat up, making an attempt to look alert and decisive.

"I thought I might have to lie awake, fighting him off, but I just went to sleep. I feel great." He stretched in surprise. "I could run for miles."

"Be careful," she warned him.

David look at her apprehensively. "Why?"

"He's lying in wait."

"Oh, I know that." He seemed to have grown up a good deal overnight. "We're not finished with him yet. And we won't be unless we *do* something."

"What *can* we do?" Jenny was at a loss.

"We've got to find out what really happened. We've got to find out how Bud died. That's the only way I can help him, the only way I can protect

62

myself – and you – and even Sarah. Bud wants to use me and we've *got* to find out why."

"It's all been triggered off by something," said Jenny slowly. She was delighted that the night's respite had strengthened David, but was apprehensive about the remainder of the day. Bud hadn't stayed away so long since he had first contacted them.

"Was it because of Dad taking up the lease?"

"More than that." She was more confident now. "Do you think it could have anything to do with Gilbert Malvin? Mum told me the Chamber of Commerce are organising this big Christmas dinner for him. Thanking him for all he's done for the community. Could that have been the trigger?"

"Why should it?"

"I don't know. But for a long time nothing happened on the quayside. It just rotted away. Now things are changing. Dad's got the lease. Gilbert Malvin's being congratulated."

David nodded. "You might be right, but there must be more. Maybe Bud's feeling even more forgotten than ever." He shivered and looked less assertive. "His spirit's been wandering for a long time. He can't rest."

Jenny gazed down at her twin thoughtfully. "You're feeling sorry for him, aren't you?"

"In a way. But I'm really scared. I can feel him waiting for me."

The twins stared at each other in silence, knowing how strong Bud was. His pent-up anger had finally boiled over.

At breakfast, Mr Golding had an announcement to make.

"The forecast says there's more snow to come and that's going to hold us up at Standard Quay. We'll never move all that junk in these conditions, so I'm going to delay the opening by a couple of weeks. It can't be helped." He paused and sighed. "We're going to have to put up with the demolition plans being brought forward as well." He frowned. "Gilbert Malvin's managed to persuade the council to knock down Standard House *and* St James's ahead of schedule, so there'll be all that mess to contend with. The demolition squad are due to arrive next week."

"Malvin *must* have influence in the right places," commented Mum. "The council never bring anything forward. They usually put it back."

"He's got influence all right. But you've got to remember what a big local benefactor Malvin is. Look how much he's given the council already. They'll do anything for him in the hope of more." Mr Golding cleared his throat and then glared at David and Jenny. "All this brings me to another point. I don't want you two messing around at Standard Quay. Know what I mean?"

Jenny and David tried to look innocent, as if they hadn't had the slightest intention of doing anything of the kind.

"Someone been complaining about us?" asked David indignantly.

Mum came to the rescue as she often did. "Mrs Bertram phoned. Something about playing around with a bike up there," she said. "They're a funny reclusive pair. I often see her in the supermarket pushing a trolley, but she keeps herself to herself. Won't pass the time of day. I've tried smiling at her, but she just stared straight through me."

"That boy who was killed," Jenny broke in, determined to capitalise on the conversation. "Was he murdered?"

A hush descended over the breakfast table.

"No," said Mr Golding firmly. "I'm sure he wasn't, but I don't know anything about it. We weren't here, were we? All your mother and I have heard is local rumour and you can't trust that."

"What *do* the rumours say?" demanded David. "Come on, Dad, tell us."

"All we know," interrupted their mother reluctantly, "is that Gilbert Malvin's brother lived in Standard House and that they quarrelled and the boy died as a result of some accident. They say Gilbert worshipped his nephew and his death broke his heart, and that's why he's a recluse. That's all we know." Mrs Golding paused and gazed at David and Jenny searchingly. "What are you two up to? Why are you so interested?" She frowned. "And what about that bike?"

David swallowed. "I found it in the shed," he said defensively. "Old-fashioned sort of thing."

"But you've got a perfectly good one of your own," protested Mrs Golding.

"I only tried it out."

"Well, you shouldn't have done. That bike belonged to the dead boy, I reckon." Mr Golding looked worried. "Mrs Bertram says Gilbert Malvin was very upset that it was ridden and now he's taken it back to the vicarage."

David nodded abruptly. He didn't want to give anything more away.

Jenny looked at her twin anxiously, hoping he wasn't going to antagonise their parents. She didn't want a row, particularly if Mum and Dad knew anything else. If they clammed up now, she and David would never find out why Bud was so angry.

"Look," said Mrs Golding. "We don't want to get on the wrong side of Mr Malvin or Mrs Bertram. We want to make a success of Standard Quay."

"I know you do," said Jenny. "We were both wrong to mess about with the bike. We're sorry."

"It's OK." Her mother obviously didn't like Mrs Bertram. "The old girl was getting all worked up and I was quite annoyed. She said David had deliberately ridden the bike at her, tried to knock her down. Well I soon saw her off on that one. I told her David's not that sort of boy. He's not a hooligan. He wouldn't dream of doing such a thing."

David went into his room and shut the door. He sat on the edge of his bed and then lay down on his back, fists clenched, determined to keep Bud out.

He had felt the pressure in his head towards the end of breakfast, felt the cloudiness coming over him, as if he couldn't remember his own name. In fact he couldn't recall anything except the two men struggling in the study at Standard House.

"*Dad*," he muttered. "*Leave him alone. Leave each other alone.*"

Momentarily, David's mind freed itself and he imagined his own family sitting round the breakfast table. But the familiar and reassuring scene was soon swamped again.

He knew he had to get help. He had to stop them killing each other. He had to get his bike and ride out into the streets, despite the snow, despite all that was at stake. If the police came his father would be arrested, but if they didn't, one of them might die. Bud knew how much the hatred and despair had built up.

David staggered to his feet, trying to throw Bud out of his mind, trying to fight back. For a fleeting moment he saw his own bedroom. For a brief second he shouted for Jenny. Then Bud closed in again.

Jenny heard him cry out and ran in from the wharf. Her parents were clearing snow and she and David had decided to help them. At the last moment, David had run up to his room to fetch his gloves.

Jenny knew she should have reacted faster, but Mum had kept her talking about old Mrs Rogers, wondering if the school's community project might decorate her flat.

"That's David," Jenny had said. "I bet you he can't find his gloves. I'll go and help him."

She knew her mother was staring after her in astonishment. Jenny didn't usually act as her brother's servant. In fact very much the opposite. But panic was filling her and she raced for the house.

As she threw open his bedroom door, Jenny saw David standing in the middle of the floor, watching something that she couldn't see. His fists were clenched, sweat was pouring down his face and his voice was husky as he shouted at her, "*I've got to get help!*"

"Help? Help for what?"

"*I can't make them stop. They're going to kill each other. I've got to get help. I'll get the bike. Find someone. Even the police. It doesn't matter now.*"

"David!" Jenny yelled. "Fight him! Fight him off!"

"*I'm not fighting,*" came Bud's voice. "*They're the ones who are fighting. Get out of my way.*"

From somewhere outside came the urgent shrilling of a bicycle bell. Jenny grabbed at David, desperate to stop him, but he pushed her back on the bed with such force that she fell off the other side, banging her head against the wall.

David didn't even look back as he ran out of the room.

He got on the ghost bike and pedalled down the track that led to Standard Quay. The cloudiness was in his mind and he knew instinctively that Bud and he were one, however much he willed against it.

David tried to fight back. He felt as if he had been forced into some small room in his mind, that this was his last stand and that Bud was already trying to break down the door.

"What do you want?"

I want to punish him.

"What's he done?"

He sent my father away. He made me die. He kept the money.

David still battled back: "What are you going to do?"

Uncle Gilbert's got to pay.

"How?"

I'm going to kill him.

"I don't understand." Then David heard a new sound inside his head, like a heart beating, faster and faster. "You mean *I'm* going to kill him, don't you? But I won't do it."

The thudding began again, resounding so loudly that he could hardly breathe.

CHAPTER TEN

The knowledge that Bud had taken David over yet again with such ease made Jenny despair. She was about to grab her bike and follow her twin, when she realised that if she didn't give her parents some kind of explanation they would be worried. She eventually tracked them down at the back of the boiler house.

"David and I have decided to go down to Standard Quay and apologise personally to Mrs Bertram. We shan't hang around afterwards."

"That's a nice idea," said Mum, red in the face from her exertions with the spade. "Good for you."

"Don't touch that bike whatever you do." Dad was less accommodating. "We've got to get on with the old – with Mrs Bertram." Then he grinned at Jenny. "But I know how you two can switch on the charm."

She set off on her bike, but the going was so tough Jenny found she had to push. She struggled on in the penetrating cold, her fingers and toes turning numb.

When David had thrown her on to the bed, she knew he had been completely taken over by Bud. David would never have treated her like that. Because of the change in him she felt completely isolated. It was a weird sensation, feeling so alone as a twin. If only she could find the reason for Bud's anger and help him. If only pigs had wings, her mother would say. The odds seemed so heavily stacked against her.

"Where are you, Dave?" she said aloud, a sob in her voice.

When Jenny arrived at Standard Quay it was as silent and as snow-bound as it had been the previous day. The sun had gone behind banked clouds and there was a shut-off, enclosed feeling to the quayside and its run-down buildings as if they formed a world of their own – a world that had stood still for too long.

Jenny gazed up at Standard House, solid and dominating, its dirty windows like blind eyes. Then she saw the front door was standing half open as it had done yesterday.

There were no lights in the vicarage but the church had something flickering at one of the windows. Could it be a candle? But why should anyone light a candle in a derelict church?

Then Jenny realised there were no tyre marks in the snow at all. It was virgin white. By the steps of

St James's, however, there was a deep skid, almost as if the ghost bike had flown to a landing.

The sudden sound of an organ broke into Jenny's troubled thoughts. Did someone still practise in the old church? Could that someone be Gilbert Malvin?

Then she heard the sound of a congregation singing and she stood rigidly still, looking up at the gargoyle in the shape of a griffin above the doors. For a moment Jenny thought the griffin winked, but it must have been some trick of the dull, flat light.

The singing made her feel that ice had entered her soul.

"Abide with me; fast falls the eventide;
The darkness deepens; Lord, with me abide!"

Putting her bike down in the snow, Jenny walked slowly across to St James's. She cried out in pain as deep cold crept up her ankles.

"When other helpers fail, and comforts flee,
Help of the helpless, O abide with me."

The singing was like an echo as if it was something that had happened a long time ago and went on vibrating down the years.

She ran up the steps and pushed at the freezing damp wood of the doors. They slowly opened.

★

Jenny saw flickering candles and a dark, insubstantial image of a congregation that shimmered, frond-like, as if they were weeds under water. They cracked and bubbled slightly and the air was damp and draughty.

"Swift to its close ebbs out life's little day;
Earth's joys grow dim, its glories pass away."

The coffin was on a trestle just below the altar step and the priest was standing beside it, misty and glimmering.

Jenny felt she could blow the scene away like snuffing out a candle. Yet, as she began to walk down the aisle, it seemed as if her feet were wading through treacle.

Dread seized her. The organ tinkled ice and she saw the mouths of the congregation stuffed full of snow. The hymn went out of tune, until it was like an old record player that needed winding.

"Change and decay in all around I see;
O thou who changest not, abide with me."

Then all the reverence disappeared, and a choir-boy began to sing.

"I'm forever blowing bubbles,
Pretty bubbles in the air."

The bubbles also came from the coffin, soaring to the rafters of the church. Jenny turned and ran, unable to take any more, her feet leaden.

Then she saw David standing at the back of the church. Bud must be in control. Was he creating all this? Was he showing her a distorted glimpse of his own past?

"I'm here to help you, Bud," Jenny yelled.

David turned and ran out of St James's, leaving her alone, gazing back down the nave of the church, watching the bubbles blowing, the organ wheezing and the choirboy singing.

"They fly so high, nearly reach the sky.
Then like my dreams they fade and die."

Suddenly Jenny found she was released and could run freely. When she glanced back again she saw the dusty church was empty and there was no sound but her own footsteps on the stone floor.

The tall dark boy was riding across the snow, pedalling furiously and skidding wildly. He wasn't David, but he was on the ghost bike. Jenny could hear shouting from Standard House, the sound of breaking glass, and the boy on the bike swooped on, perilously nearing the dry dock.

Suddenly he swerved, plunging over the edge, his scream like a bird cawing. Then the sky was dark with rooks as they flew over the edge of the dock, wheeling and diving in a wild cacophony of sound which was abruptly cut off.

Silence returned and Jenny saw that, once again,

there were no tracks in the snow, not even by the church. It was all white again and completely unsullied.

She watched Boris appear from the direction of the graveyard. He ran up the steps of St James's and turned snarling at the top. Then he padded inside.

"Where's David? Where's my brother?" she screamed, but only the wind replied, darting into the old buildings, making an eerie whistling sound that came and went unpredictably. Snow flumes blew around her and she felt the searing cold.

Jenny waded towards the shed. She was sure that David would be in there. She *had* to be sure.

But when she opened the door, there was no one there at all. The bike wasn't clamped to the workbench either. It had disappeared. She gazed around in the gloom but there was nothing.

Could David be in Standard House? Would she have to force herself to explore its dark spaces? Jenny stood in the shed, using all her will to reach her twin, to try and detect where he might be.

Outside, she heard the cawing of a rook. Then the door of the shed was flung open.

CHAPTER ELEVEN

A man stood in the doorway. He was tall, with long white hair that fell on to the collar of his frayed dark suit. His clean-shaven face was a pale oval, with high cheekbones. It was difficult to guess his age, but Jenny thought he might be in his seventies. His eyes were a milky blue, and when he spoke his voice was as thin as his lips.

"Miss Golding?"

"Who are you?"

"I'm Gilbert Malvin. I'm afraid your brother has had a slight accident. But it's not serious." He spoke very precisely yet there was also a slight hesitancy, as if he didn't speak very often. "Your brother's in the vicarage now, being looked after by my housekeeper."

"Where did he have this accident?"

"Mrs Bertram found him in the graveyard. He'd tripped over a headstone and knocked himself out."

"How long was he lying there?" Jenny was horrified. Was this Bud's work?

"Not long I think. He was calling out and she heard him, thank God. Another half an hour out there in these conditions . . ." Gilbert Malvin paused. "The young man didn't seem to be able to get to his feet. There was a cut on his head but we can't find any other injuries, and Mrs Bertram used to be a nurse. Your brother refused to allow us to call a doctor. Of course we should have overruled him but he became quite hysterical." Gilbert Malvin's original halting words had turned into a flood. "You'd better come with me," he said unhappily.

Jenny followed Gilbert Malvin across the quay to the vicarage. Now there were a good number of footprints criss-crossing the snow. Paw prints too. Then she saw Boris sitting on an upturned crate, his one eye watching her beadily.

Gilbert Malvin climbed the front steps slowly and unsteadily and she wondered when he had last gone out. His skin was chalky white and he wheezed badly.

He opened the front door of the vicarage with a shaking hand and they entered the stuffy hallway that smelt of dusty coats and stale food.

Sarah came running up to Jenny eagerly. "Have you come to play?" she asked.

"I don't think so," Jenny replied nervously as Boris brushed past her. He had a faintly earthy smell and she was once again unpleasantly reminded of the grave.

"It's not fair," said Sarah. "I'm lonely here. Just like that boy." She paused. "David's OK. He doesn't need a doctor."

"Be quiet, Sarah." Jenny caught a look of pain on Gilbert Malvin's face which he quickly covered up with irritation.

"Did the boy hurt David?" Sarah asked.

"You don't know what you're talking about." Gilbert Malvin walked past her unsteadily.

David was slumped in an old armchair that looked incongruous in the rambling kitchen, which was an unexpectedly cheerful place compared with the oppressive and over-furnished hallway.

There was a fire glowing in the grate and Boris was now lying in front of it, basking. There was a large Welsh dresser, an old-fashioned range and a wooden table in the centre of the room.

"I'll leave you with Mrs Bertram," said Gilbert Malvin. "I'm not feeling myself."

Neither am I, thought Jenny as she gazed at the cut just above David's eyebrow.

"Are you OK?" she asked.

He nodded.

"What happened?"

"I was on the bike," he whispered as the kettle began to whistle and Mrs Bertram turned to switch it off. Sarah watched the twins curiously, sitting on the table, swinging her legs. "When I got here it tipped me off outside the church and went down the passage to the graveyard. When I followed I think I saw Bud. He's tall and dark."

"I've seen him too," said Jenny, but she decided against telling David exactly what happened.

"He was staring down at a gravestone covered in ivy and brambles. Then he moved along to a new grave next door. He started laughing. I stood beside him . . ." David began to shake.

He told Jenny what the inscription had read: "Gilbert Malvin. Died December 12th, 1997 RIP"

"But that's today!" cried Jenny.

"I know, and then I fell over and hit my head and Bud laughed even harder." David paused, looking up at Jenny as if he was willing her to believe him. "When I came to I saw another inscription. It said *Winifred Summers. Died February 19th, 1886. RIP.*" David paused for breath. "So it couldn't have been Mr Malvin's, could it?"

"Of course not," snapped Jenny brusquely. "It's all an illusion."

"What's an illusion?" asked Sarah, who had been listening to their conversation.

"Something you see but isn't there," said Jenny.

"Can this boy –"

"Will you be quiet, Sarah." Mrs Bertram wheeled round on her, speaking far more angrily than Gilbert Malvin had. "There *is* no boy. There's only sadness – and something that has its own echoes."

"I don't know what you mean," began Sarah.

"When there's been a very big event somewhere

it leaves vibrations down the years. That's all that's happening."

Then Jenny saw that the expression on Mrs Bertram's face had suddenly changed. She was gazing down at David in concern.

"Go away, Bud," he whispered.

Boris got to his feet, walked slowly towards him and then jumped up into David's lap, purring. Her twin made no attempt to push the cat away.

"We've *got* to talk." Jenny appealed to Mrs Bertram. "My brother's being driven out of his mind by all this." As she spoke she realised how accurately she had described the situation.

Mrs Bertram glared at her. "This is nonsense," she rapped out, as if attempting to brush away what was happening, just as Jenny had once tried to do. "Absolute nonsense. You both came here trespassing in the first place, taking something that wasn't yours –"

"We didn't want the bike," said Jenny sharply. "We didn't want it at all. Don't you understand? It belonged to Bud. Now Bud's got to my brother. He's controlling him."

"How does he do that?" asked Sarah, and then waited to be shouted at by her grandmother. To her surprise, however, Mrs Bertram said nothing at all.

"I don't know. He gets inside him. Look at David now." Jenny was losing all control. "He's possessed. Can't you see? He's possessed by Bud and he won't go away." She burst into tears and Sarah jumped down from the table, throwing her arms around Jenny's waist and trying to comfort her.

As she did this, Boris stretched, yawned and then jumped off David's lap, returning lazily to the fire. His empty eye socket was lit by the flames and Jenny shuddered as she saw what she thought was a deep, dark, gleaming pool.

"We'll help get rid of Bud," said Sarah. "Won't we, Gran?"

Mrs Bertram shook her head, suddenly looking much older. "I don't know what to say," she muttered. "I knew wrong had been done. But I never believed – could never have believed that – " She broke off. "Surely time heals? I – "

But Mrs Bertram never finished what she was saying as David stood up and Bud's husky voice spat out vindictively, "*Time doesn't heal. Time never heals.*"

"It should do." Mrs Bertram's voice was weak and unsteady.

"*Uncle Gilbert's going to pay.*"

David sank back into his chair again and closed his eyes.

"He needs rest," she said vaguely.

"We've got to find out what Bud wants." Jenny glanced down at her twin, terrified to see that he looked like a used and empty husk. "But you're right. We're not going to find out anything until he's had some rest. I reckon that if David's exhausted, Bud has to make a terrific effort to come through. He needs my brother's mind and body. He needs him fit and well." Jenny turned to Mrs Bertram. "You've got to help me. Why *does* Bud want revenge? Why is he so angry? And why *now*?"

Mrs Bertram was silent. Then she wiped her hands on her apron, sat down heavily and began to fiddle with the sugar bowl.

"David's in terrible danger —" Jenny began again in mounting desperation. "It's not his fault Bud's got this hatred for Gilbert Malvin."

She wondered how far she should go without totally alarming Mrs Bertram and turning her into an enemy. Jenny knew she had to try to get her confidence.

"Uncle Gilbert's got to help, Gran," put in Sarah.

They heard a light step on the stair and then Gilbert Malvin came into the room, looking white and strained.

David sat up, his eyes wide open, and Bud said, "*Dad and I are going to France.*"

Jenny took a few paces towards her brother, seeing the hostile glint in his eye but not able to stop herself trying to reach him, however terrified she felt.

"Fight back, Dave," she whispered. "You've got to fight back."

But David's lips parted in a sneer.

"*You mustn't go*," muttered Gilbert Malvin, confused and hardly able to cope. He staggered slightly, looking round him in despair. "*You stay with me, Bud. You've got to stay with me.*"

"It's all right, Gilbert," said Mrs Bertram. "The boy's sick. He doesn't know what he's saying."

David was on his feet now, shouting in Bud's husky voice, and Jenny knew that the past had come alive again.

"*We're going*," rasped Bud. "*You can't stop him. Or me.*"

David put his head down and ran, pushing past Gilbert Malvin who clutched ineffectively at him and then set off in unsteady pursuit, followed by Jenny. Mrs Bertram grabbed Sarah and held her close.

Reaching the open front door of the vicarage, Jenny saw David racing through the snow towards Standard House with Gilbert Malvin stumbling along behind him. Then she saw a face at the first-floor window.

"*I'm coming, Dad*," yelled Bud as David pushed open the front door and disappeared inside.

Something shifted and Jenny was not quite sure whether the change occurred in her mind or to the actual scene around her.

She had run from the vicarage steps and had overtaken Gilbert Malvin, but when she looked back he wasn't there. In front of her, a younger man was closing the front door of Standard House.

Jenny wrenched it open again, and saw a flight of stairs with a threadbare carpet. The man was running up them with considerable speed and she hesitated, not knowing whether to follow.

The hall was lit by warm electric light and the walls were covered with pictures of ships – galleons and steamers and fishing trawlers and yachts and liners and . . .

"*When are we going, Dad?*"

"*Right away.*"

Their voices, like those in the church, were distant, uneven and blurred.

"*You're not going anywhere,*" said another voice that was just as indistinct. "*You're not going away with that money or my nephew. I* can't *let you go, Tom. You know I can't.*"

Jenny realised that the young man she had seen run into Standard House was Gilbert Malvin. She experienced the sensation of walking round a bend, as if she had been lost and had now regained her sense of direction. But where was David in all this confusion of time?

She began to climb the stairs which were mistily misshapen. When she reached the landing everything was at the wrong angle like a crazy house in a funfair. The levels were all out of alignment, the door frames were bent, the ceilings and floors were lumpy as if they were made of cotton wool.

The blurred sounds were coming from a room to her left and Jenny hurried towards wafting grey light. She felt a blast of cold air and smelt raw earth.

When she gazed inside she saw a study with more pictures of ships on the wall, a giant globe near the bookcase and a desk against which two tall men were silently struggling. A dark-haired boy was trying ineffectively to pull them apart.

As Jenny slowly entered the room the earth smell intensified and the shapes of the struggling figures and the furnishings of the study became insubstantial and shadowy. The air seemed charged with electricity and there was a buzzing sound, as if someone had forgotten to switch off a television set after the final programme had ended.

Firmly, the dark boy was pushed aside by the combatants and he landed on his back at her feet on the landing. His touch was soft, like a feather, and when she gazed down at Bud's face she saw him properly for the first time.

He was deeply tanned, with a mane of black hair and eyes that were glazed with fear. Bud was tall, like his father and uncle, but his build was slight, and although he was wiry he would have been quite unable to separate the two men.

Bud struggled to his feet. "*You've got to stop. If you don't I'll go for help. I'll get the police –*"

But Tom and Gilbert only fought on.

"*I'm going!*" His voice sounded as if it was bubbling under water now. The walls bent towards Jenny and the floor became pulpy and shifting.

Bud turned and ran downstairs, half sobbing and shouting indistinctly, "*They'll kill each other. Someone help me.*"

Jenny raced down the soft stairs after Bud. In her panic she fell the last few steps, landing on her stomach, winded. She knew what was going to happen. Everything was going to go horribly wrong. Then she heard the distant ringing of a bicycle bell.

CHAPTER TWELVE

David was walking across the snow towards her. He looked beaten and the cut over his eye was a ragged tear.

"I thought you'd gone in the house," Jenny said, dragging herself to her feet to gaze back at the uncarpeted staircase. There were no pictures on the walls, no warm glow of electricity. Just darkness and the all too familiar smell of earth.

"I got to the door," David said. "But Bud left me behind."

"He went back," replied Jenny. "It must be so terrible for him, so painful. How many times does he have to do this? It's like the past is constantly replaying for him – as if he can never leave that awful time." For the first time she realised she was almost sorry for Bud and his dreadful plight.

"You mean he *lives* in the past?" David asked incredulously.

"Possession is the only way he can make things happen. I've got this feeling that he can't leave Standard Quay or ever be at rest because the past – his past – isn't resolved." She told David about what she had seen in the church and later in the house. "I can only just see what Bud sees. But I reckon it goes on repeating itself, time after time after time. No wonder he's so angry. No wonder he wants to take revenge."

"Through me," said David mournfully. "That's really great, isn't it? Poor old Bud. What about poor old me? I'm just his innocent victim. Just a passing body to hijack."

Jenny gazed at her brother steadily. "If we can't understand Bud, then you'll never be safe."

"Just don't be too sorry for him, that's all," David muttered.

"Wait a minute," said Jenny. "I'm sure I saw Gilbert Malvin's younger self go into Standard House, so where's his real self? As he is today?"

David gazed at his sister uneasily. He wasn't sure he could cope with any more. He felt as if he was only awake in certain parts of a story and the rest of the time he wasn't around. As a result, he was finding connections hard to make. "I saw him going into Standard House. At least I think I did. He wasn't changed at all."

Then they both heard the cry of pain from upstairs.

"We're going to have to go up," said David. His face was set and Jenny's heart went out to him. Never, in all their ghostly adventures, had her twin been under such a threat.

"Suppose Bud's up there?"

"I don't feel him but that doesn't mean much. He comes like lightning." They hurried up the creaking staircase to the first landing.

"That was the room they were fighting in," Jenny said.

They hurried into the dusty, empty study to find Gilbert Malvin lying on the floor and breathing raggedly. His face was a nasty shade of blue.

"Haven't you done enough?" whispered David, and Jenny knew he wasn't talking to her. He was telling Bud to leave them alone.

Would his spirit ever be at peace? wondered Jenny as she gazed down at the old man wheezing at her feet. Even if David was able to miraculously reject him, would Bud wait until another boy came along with the sight and try to possess him too?

Gilbert Malvin muttered something they couldn't understand.

"One of us has got to go to the vicarage and ring for an ambulance," said David.

Jenny tried to work out who should go. If David went, would Bud try to prevent him reaching the phone? If he stayed would Bud get inside him again? Jenny dithered, unable to make the decision.

In the end, David took the initiative. "I'll go for the phone. I don't want to stay with Malvin on my own. Just in case."

Jenny nodded, knowing exactly what he meant.

As David raced back down the stairs she was left alone with Gilbert Malvin whose breathing seemed to be getting worse.

"Hang on." She took his hand gently and encouragingly. "The ambulance will be here soon."

He muttered something and then said more clearly, "I can't go now. Not with his spirit so troubled."

So he did understand, Jenny thought triumphantly. But did he also realise that Bud wanted revenge?

"How can we release his spirit?" she asked hesitantly.

"Tom. My brother Tom."

"Do you know where he lives?"

"Spain," he whispered. Gilbert Malvin seemed to be getting weaker.

"Is that all you know?"

"Mutual friends. Mrs Bertram – my address book."

"He never came back?"

"Never. Tragedy. As much my fault as Tom's. We failed Bud." His voice was no more than a whisper and the wheezing was more pronounced.

"If we find Tom, what are the chances of Bud's spirit being put to rest?"

"He blames me. Loss of his father. His own

death. If I die – he'll be pleased." The old man choked back a sob.

"You're *not* going to die," said Jenny firmly.

"Maybe better. Bud would like it that way." Gilbert Malvin's voice was very faint now.

"He can't be that horrible." But as she spoke Jenny remembered that at least Bud hadn't used David as his weapon. He hadn't needed to. It was the shock of realisation that might kill Malvin.

"Good boy," whispered Gilbert Malvin tenderly. "Worshipped his father."

"Like you worshipped Bud?" asked Jenny gently.

"Bud was – all I had. Tom couldn't take him away."

Jenny frowned, but before she could say any more she heard the sound of footsteps on the stairs and froze.

"Who is it?" she called.

"It's me," said Mrs Bertram as she arrived with blankets and a hot water bottle. Boris was at her heels in dog-like devotion, stretching and rubbing against her legs.

"Your brother's outside, waiting to direct the ambulance."

Jenny immediately felt panic-stricken. If David was alone that would be fine. But suppose he wasn't? Suppose Bud was back?

"I'll go and help him," she said and ran out of the

study and down the stairs of Standard House. As she hurried out into the snow, Jenny felt something soft brush her leg and she almost fell, kicking out to try to save herself. She just managed to stay upright as she heard the yowl of pain.

Jenny looked down to see Boris's yellow eye glaring at her. Then he ran back towards the vicarage, spitting and howling.

She waited for the ambulance on the main road. The access to Standard Quay was through a network of narrow roads and it would be easy for the crew to get lost. Besides, she wanted to stay clear of David, at least for the time being.

Within a few minutes Jenny could see blue lights flashing and hear a siren wailing. The road had been cleared of snow, but the surface was still treacherous and the ambulance approached cautiously until she flagged it down.

As she started to give directions, the driver told her to get in and show them herself.

"We've been lost round these old dockland areas before," he explained. "It's like a maze."

Jenny guided the ambulance to the snow-covered quayside and the front of Standard House. As the vehicle pulled up and she was about to get out, she saw David standing outside.

His face was twisted with Bud's rage.

Boris was sitting in the shadows, spitting

viciously. Jenny felt surrounded by enemies.

"*This isn't Standard House,*" Bud shouted angrily. "*You take another left, another right and –* "

"Don't listen to him," said Jenny quickly. "Your patient is on the first floor. Please hurry."

"*She's having you on. She's stupid. She doesn't know what's what.*" Bud's husky voice was scornful. "*Never rely on women.*"

The two paramedics looked at each other in bewilderment. "Now who's playing games?" asked the driver, looking from Jenny to David and then back again.

"This boy's not well." Jenny was getting desperate. "Mr Malvin's had a heart attack. He's up on the first floor."

"*Let him die,*" snarled Bud. "*He drove my father away. He let me die. Now it's his turn.*"

"Do you see what I mean?" demanded Jenny.

The driver nodded. "The boy looks like you, miss. Is he a relation?"

"No." Jenny got out, wondering what Bud would do. Might he attack her?

But instead David ran off towards the vicarage, yelling over his shoulder, "*Let him die. For what he did.*"

"That boy's a bad case," said the paramedic as he and his colleague pulled out the stretcher and made their way up the stairs of Standard House. "Is he under medication?"

"Yes," replied Jenny as steadily as she could. "He's been mentally ill for quite a time now. But he's being cared for."

"I hope so. He seemed very disturbed."

You can say that again, thought Jenny.

CHAPTER THIRTEEN

As the ambulance drove away with Gilbert Malvin safely inside, Mrs Bertram walked back to the vicarage with Jenny. There was a closeness between them now, a bonding made from crisis. "I'd have gone with Gilbert if it hadn't been for Sarah," she said. "But I've got to keep an eye on her with all this going on." Mrs Bertram didn't specify what and it was difficult to know whether she was just reacting to strange events or was actually trying to accept Bud's unquiet spirit.

Jenny nodded comfortingly. "They'll take good care of him at the hospital."

"This Bud – is he ever going to leave us in peace?"

Jenny was surprised. So Mrs Bertram *had* come to believe in what they were up against. "Only when he finds peace himself," she said, and then could have kicked herself for sounding so glib.

"And how is he going to do that, may I ask?"

"I've got an idea. But I don't know how to put it into action."

"Well?" Mrs Bertram was obviously anxious to find a solution.

"Do you think his father's alive?" asked Jenny.

"I've no idea."

"Mr Malvin wanted you to go through his address book and try to find some mutual friends who might know where Tom is."

"I could try."

"It's urgent," insisted Jenny.

"I appreciate that. But what if we can't find Tom Malvin? Or suppose he's dead?"

"We'll face that when we have to, but we need to work fast. And now you've got to tell me what happened that day at Standard House – when Bud was killed."

"It's all second-hand information. All I know is what Mr Malvin told me." Mrs Bertram sounded afraid of saying too much.

"That'll do for a start," said Jenny grimly.

As Mrs Bertram opened the kitchen door, she started back with a cry of alarm. Jenny pushed past her and saw David playing a game of snakes and ladders on the floor with Sarah.

"I got a bit confused," he said. "I don't know where the bike is."

"That's locked away," said Mrs Bertram firmly. "Locked away for good."

"So I came in here and found Sarah on her own. She was a bit frightened so we started playing this game." He gazed up at Mrs Bertram, childlike and vulnerable. "I hope that was OK."

She gazed back at him suspiciously, but Jenny could see that her brother was genuinely confused.

She looked at her watch. Five o'clock. Jenny decided to ring her parents and tell them that she and David had gone over to a friend's house and might be a little while yet. It was almost true. After all, Mrs Bertram was a friend now, wasn't she? Sort of.

David, Sarah and Jenny sat round the wooden table in the kitchen while Mrs Bertram produced scones, buns and two kinds of home-made cake as well as a large brown pot of strong and refreshing tea.

As they ate, she hesitantly told them about the Malvin family tragedy. Jenny kept watching David's eyes, but if Bud was about he was keeping a remarkably low profile.

"Tom Malvin ran the shipyard but gradually he went bankrupt. There just wasn't enough work any longer, but Tom was extravagant and a bad manager. His wife had left him for another man some years before so he and Bud had got very close. Too close. Gilbert was a lawyer, a church-goer and a real pillar of society. The Malvin family were respected by the local community, and that respect was deeply prized by Gilbert. At the time of the tragedy he was the mayor." Mrs Bertram paused. "I'm telling you all this not because I have to, but because we need to pool our resources. I've never believed in the spirit world before –" She looked at David, but his expression didn't change. He remained clear-eyed and innocent.

The innocent victim, thought Jenny, the hurt spreading inside her so much that she could hardly bear it any longer. She loved David so much. Whatever was she going to do? What were they all going to do, particularly if Tom Malvin was dead or couldn't be found.

Mrs Bertram continued, talking quickly now as if she wanted to finish her explanation as fast as she could.

"Tom got so desperate that he robbed a bank and returned to Standard House with a considerable sum of money. Gilbert found out – and was naturally horrified, particularly when he discovered that Tom was going to take the money – and Bud – and start a new life abroad." Mrs Bertram paused reflectively and then she said abruptly, "I don't know which was worse for Gilbert, the idea of losing Bud, or Tom blackening the Malvin family name. When the two brothers fought, Bud was killed riding for help on that wretched bike. He skidded in the snow and fell into the dry dock. The doctor told Gilbert that he died instantly. Tom ran off, just as he had planned, but without his beloved son – or the money." Mrs Bertram began to blink back the tears. "Gilbert kept it all. He couldn't bring himself to admit what had happened, to bring the family name into disrepute, so he decided to use his position as mayor to give it away, funding local charities. He did this in bits and pieces over a period of years, and naturally received a good deal of praise. The police never suspected either of the Malvins and the bank raider's identity remained a mystery.

"But Gilbert found it difficult to live with his conscience and he became a recluse. That was when he employed me as his housekeeper and over the years we've become very fond of each other." Mrs Bertram gazed at her granddaughter with a wry smile. "As Sarah told you." Then she continued again. "I'm glad he was able to confide in me. But this dinner that's being organised by the Chamber of Commerce to honour him has lain on his conscience. Badly. Nevertheless, he'll have to go through with it."

"Because of the family name?" asked David.

"There've been Malvins as shipwrights here for hundreds of years. They have always been scrupulously honest. It's almost a sacred task for Gilbert to protect that – just like Bud's memory. All he had left of him was the bike. He had it repaired after the accident and there isn't a day when he doesn't visit it. He couldn't bear to see the grave; the bike's always been Bud's shrine."

"And is now his weapon," said Jenny quietly.

Mrs Bertram's eyes met hers. "Now I've told you the Malvin family secret – what are you going to do with it?" Her voice trembled.

"Nothing," said Jenny and David simultaneously.

"The money's Mr Malvin's responsibility," said Jenny. "It was never anything to do with Bud." Then she turned to Mrs Bertram. "We've *got* to help him."

"We've got to stop him, you mean," said David with quiet desperation.

"The point is," said Jenny, "that Bud feels abandoned. He blames his Uncle Gilbert for that and wants him to suffer."

"Why has Bud suddenly appeared now?" asked Sarah, puzzled.

"Because Gilbert Malvin's had some recent good luck, hasn't he? He and Mrs Bertram are in love and then there's the Chamber of Commerce dinner," explained David warily. "Bud knows that Gilbert used the stolen money and now he's being honoured for it. He thinks Gilbert's a hypocrite. Let's face it, he just –" David paused, catching Jenny's warning glance. "Bud's just out of control," he finished lamely.

"I don't think it's *just* the dinner, or even Mrs Bertram making Gilbert Malvin happy," said Jenny. "Those two things have certainly made Bud furiously angry, but without David he wouldn't have been able to express it. My brother's psychic. Like I am. It all started when David touched the bike. Bud had a way of communicating at last."

Mrs Bertram gave them both a doubtful look. She was obviously finding everything increasingly hard to accept.

"We've got to find his dad. Maybe he'll be able to make Bud stop," said Sarah.

"He may." David was doubtful. "*If* we can find him, which seems pretty unlikely."

"Wasn't there any contact between the brothers after Tom left?" asked Jenny.

"Not to my knowledge," said Mrs Bertram, getting stiffly to her feet. "I'm going to phone the hospital and see how Gilbert is. Then I'll start looking through his address book. I think you two should go home now or your parents are going to – "

"Wait a minute," broke in David suddenly. "I've got another idea – and I think it might work."

Mrs Bertram, Jenny and Sarah gazed at him curiously.

"A better idea than tracing Tom Malvin?" demanded Jenny suspiciously, wondering if David was being influenced by Bud again.

"It's got to be got rid of," he said stubbornly. "Whether we find Tom Malvin or not."

"What has?"

"The bike."

"Gilbert would never agree to that," snapped Mrs Bertram.

"I think he would," said Sarah with her usual frankness. "He doesn't want anyone else hurt, does he?"

Mrs Bertram sighed as if she no longer trusted her own decisions. "Maybe you're right, my dear," she admitted. "But how can we get rid of the thing?"

"Chuck it in the river," said David boldly. "If we get rid of Bud's weapon, maybe we'll get rid of Bud. In fact I'll go and do it right now." He got up, but Jenny intervened.

"You can't go alone," she said. "I'm coming with you." She wasn't sure that David was right but she also thought the experiment was worth trying. Would Bud be so powerful without his bike? Or would he be twice as angry if they threw it in the river?

"So am I." Sarah looked at her grandmother challengingly. "And no one's going to stop me."

"We'll all go," said Mrs Bertram. "In fact, I'll push the bike myself." She seemed quite enthusiastic now. "I'm sure Gilbert will understand." She produced a key from her pocket. "It's locked up in what used to be the old pantry. I'll go and get it."

But as Mrs Bertram rose to her feet, Boris began to snarl and spit.

"Now what's the matter with him?" she asked impatiently.

CHAPTER FOURTEEN

This is too easy, thought Jenny, as the four of them walked through the snow, past the dry dock and down to the quay. Was David right? By destroying Bud's weapon could they really banish him? And what about the search for Tom Malvin? Then Jenny realised how lucky Mrs Bertram would be to find him. Maybe it *was* better to dump the bike. What's Bud doing? What's he waiting for? she wondered.

The Thames flowed darkly past on the full tide, the surface looking swollen and hostile. A tug hooted and another forged downstream, towing barges comfortingly lit from stem to stern.

David was thinking much the same as his sister. Where's Bud? Surely he can't want his bike destroyed? They exchanged nervous glances, and at that moment, as if their lack of confidence had let him in, Bud returned.

At first David just felt a coldness in his ankles, but it spread like lightning, shooting up into his waist and then to his chin. The coldness turned to ice as it entered David's head, freezing his senses, numbing him completely. He was no longer in control. He no longer had any willpower. Bud had arrived, as swiftly as the tide.

David seized the bike from Mrs Bertram, wrenching it out of her hands, and was on the saddle in seconds. The chuckle came and Jenny knew with deadly certainty that Bud was back. He had caught them in the very act of trying to destroy his bike.

"We're going to find your father, Bud," Jenny yelled as David pedalled off into the darkness, but there was no reply.

She gazed hopelessly after her twin, terror gripping her. Why had the bike headed back towards the dry dock?

Jenny tried to run after David and then remembered she had ridden over to Standard Quay on her own bike.

"Where are you going?" cried the distraught Mrs Bertram.

"To help David."

"I'm coming too," yelled Sarah.

"You're not!" Mrs Bertram made a grab at her granddaughter but she dodged and raced away after Jenny.

Grabbing her bike, Jenny waited reluctantly for Sarah, knowing that she couldn't leave her wandering about the quayside on her own.

"I'll go on the saddlebag," Sarah said.

"I'll never support you," wailed Jenny. "Not in all this snow."

"Pedal hard!" Sarah commanded. "Just get on with it."

Sarah jumped up, the bike wobbled and Jenny stood up on the pedals. Somehow they began to make slow progress.

David was battling hopelessly against Bud's will. As they rode, Bud chuckled, the sound mounting in threat and menace.

David felt that he was strapped tight to the bike, could feel Bud's strength propelling him on, the speed increasing all the time as they seemed to hover rather than ride over the deep snow.

We're going to the dock. The dock. The dock. The dock, chanted Bud's voice in his head. However hard David struggled mentally, Bud's domination drew tightly over him. He was not able to find the least chink in his powerful armour.

The dock. The dock.

They were speeding past Standard House now, and then turning back towards the river.

"Don't hurt me, Bud," David pleaded. He had never been so afraid in his life. "You've made us fight you. There's nothing else we could have done. You don't even give your uncle a fair hearing."

I'll always hate Uncle Gilbert. Always. Always.

"He can't be completely to blame."

You don't know. You don't understand. You'll never understand.

They were nearing the edge of the dock now and its surrounding tin fence looked flimsier than ever.

This is the dock, said Bud. *Now you're going to see what it's like – to be DEAD!*

David fought back, and felt the mental grip loosen a fraction. But it was momentary and almost immediately Bud tightened up again.

Standing up on the pedals with Sarah a dead weight behind her, Jenny watched in horror as David's bike neared the dock.

"He's going to kill him," she screamed and as David hurtled towards the fence in the baleful milky light of the full moon, Jenny could see her twin's face was twisted in terror.

"Don't, Bud," she yelled. "It's not fair. He's done nothing to you."

"He's just trying to scare him, that's all." Sarah tried to be reassuring but failed.

"Of course he's not. He's going to kill David for trying to destroy the bike. Can't you see?"

Then they saw Mrs Bertram running towards the dock, moving faster than they could ever have imagined. Gasping for breath, she stood directly in front of the bike as it sped towards her.

★

Mrs Bertram screamed, ducked and then threw herself sideways. Jenny and Sarah gasped in amazement as the bike rose in the air and, silhouetted against the moon, flew from one side of the dock to the other, whilst Bud's devilish chuckling resounded across Standard Quay.

The bike hit the other side of the dock with a juddering and a screaming of metal and for a moment Jenny thought David was going to come off. His hands left the handlebars but then, to her horrified fascination, she saw them pushed forward, as if someone was forcing them down.

"There you are," said Sarah triumphantly. "I told you he was only playing."

"Some playing," muttered Jenny, as the bike sped on down the quay, dodging the car wrecks and then going even faster past the church and the vicarage and on to the snow-covered track that led back to the Goldings' garden centre.

David still fought Bud, their wills locked together, bending one way and then the other.

"Stop the bike," insisted David.

I'll never stop.

Now that he had stopped pleading with Bud and was trying to use more authority, he thought he might make more headway. Bud was a bully, and like all bullies he had to be confronted.

★

Jenny and Sarah rounded the corner on to the track. Jenny thought the muscles in her legs would burst with all the effort she was making. The pain was intense, the bike a dead weight. Then Jenny forgot all her misery when she saw what was happening between David and Bud.

The bike was stationary and shuddering on a bridge over a small creek which flowed into the Thames. Brakes locked tight, the pedals sometimes moved slightly in one direction and then in the other. Occasionally the bell shrilled, rather as if it was signalling a new round in the battle of the wills.

David's arms and legs were rigid as if he was in an iron grip, and the veins stood out on his forehead as he fought.

Within a metre of him, the swollen Thames lashed by, the dark water vicious and swirling. Slowly the bike began to lean towards the torrent.

"No, Bud – don't do it. Just leave him," yelled Jenny.

"He won't do anything," said Sarah stubbornly, determined not to believe in Bud's ferocity.

David knew he had lost yet again. He gripped the bike's handlebars as it leaned over to an angle of forty-five degrees.

"Don't do it, Bud," Jenny repeated. "Please don't do it."

The bike leant over at an even more alarming angle, and she knew that if her brother did fall into the river he wouldn't stand a chance. The tide was going out now and would sweep him away. Besides, the cold would soon get to him. Did Bud *really* want that?

"Don't plead with him," hissed Sarah. "Fight him, Jenny. Fight him till he stops." Her voice was hard. She had at last realised that Bud was no longer playing games.

Suddenly Mrs Bertram was beside them, panting and gasping, horrified at what she saw. "Let me appeal to him," she insisted.

Sarah, however, quickly intervened. "I don't think you should, Gran. He hates you."

"I've done nothing," she protested.

"Yes, you have. You're in love with his uncle. You're making Uncle Gilbert happy – and that's the last thing Bud wants."

"Stop, Bud!" shouted Jenny with much more authority and anger in her voice. "If you don't I'm not going to help find your father, and neither is anyone else. Mrs Bertram was going to make some calls and see if she can trace him, but if you hurt David she won't. Will you?"

"Of course I won't," said Mrs Bertram angrily. "I won't lift a finger to help you if *anything* happens to that boy."

An enormous black-headed gull appeared out of

nowhere and a tug hooted farther down the river. Flying just above them the gull gave a raucous cry. Then Jenny heard Bud's voice in her mind.

He doesn't want me.

"He will when he knows what's happened. That you're alone and trapped."

He doesn't care. He never cared.

"You were dead," yelled Jenny. "What else could your father do but run and go on running? If he'd stayed for the funeral he might have been caught and put in prison for years."

I'm in prison.

"Do you want to see him?" Jenny demanded.

Bud was silent, but the bike righted itself, plunged over the bridge and sped away down the track.

"Don't leave me," whispered Mrs Bertram. "I don't want to be on my own."

"I'll stay with you, Gran," said Sarah, jumping off the saddlebag. "I'll look after you."

Jenny began to pedal after David. Without Sarah, the bike was much lighter but her legs were so stiff now that she could hardly move them.

Then she felt a slight surge of optimism. Maybe she *had* reached Bud. Maybe he was going to see David safely home.

CHAPTER FIFTEEN

David was rigid as the bike sped down the track by the river. His hands were locked on to the handlebars again, and although his legs pumped up and down on the pedals he was putting no effort into the action at all. Bud was doing all the work. Bud hadn't gone. He was still with him.

The battle of wills had flattened out and David was deeply relieved that Bud had decided to suspend his terrible punishment. Did he really want to see his father after all?

Above David a torrent of clouds raced across the face of the full moon. He could feel Bud lodged in his mind again, draining him of resolution.

Then the bike took a left-hand turn, skimming over an even narrower snow-covered track. David knew where they were going and his anxiety increased. They were speeding along beside Gatlin Creek, heading for Gatlin Mire, one of the few remaining areas of marsh. He could see that the tide had drained out and all that was left was thick, oozing mud and the hulks of old coal barges.

Suddenly the bike jarred to a halt. Bud's grip had gone and David went flying over the handlebars into the snow, striking his shoulder painfully on an old wooden spar and rolling down the bank of the creek to the soft mud below.

Bud's chuckling was the only sound David heard as he hit the slime and began to sink into the soft, clinging ooze.

As Jenny pedalled furiously she was horrified to see the bike hurtling towards her, skimming along the track, its wheels barely touching the snow. David was nowhere to be seen and the bike had no apparent rider. Yet it was heading straight for her, weaving unerringly from right to left and left to right again to keep her on target.

In the end, Jenny came to a screeching halt, sliding into some icicle-hung bushes and the bike rattled past her.

"Where's David?" she yelled. "What have you done to my brother?"

I fed him to the fishes, came the giggling, teasing voice in her mind.

"Where is he? Tell me or you won't see your dad." Jenny's thoughts pounded at Bud and his bike abruptly stopped. She knew this was the only hold she had over him.

He's up the creek. The chuckling began again, hurting the inside of her head. Jenny could hardly believe what Bud had said, for she knew exactly where he meant. Gatlin Creek was a place everyone kept away from.

113

★

For a while David thrashed about desperately, but the more he struggled the deeper he sank, and soon he was up to his waist in the mud and still sinking. The slightest movement and the stuff gripped him tighter in its cold, sloppy embrace, just as Bud had gripped his mind.

David knew his only hope lay in the rotten joist of the old jetty that he had managed to grip. But try as he might, he couldn't drag himself up any further. The mud clung to him tightly and his numb hands were losing contact with the slippery wood.

Why was Bud so vicious? he wondered. Didn't he have any mercy? Then he remembered that he had taken Bud's weapon and tried to destroy it. The bike was still his most precious possession.

"David!"

He heard Jenny's voice and felt a surge of hope. "I'm over here!"

She slammed down her bike and ran to the edge of the creek.

"Over here!" he yelled.

"Where?"

"By the jetty."

Jenny was on the bank, peering out into the darkness, finally seeing her brother clinging to one of the joists.

"I'm coming."

"Don't!" he yelled. "All the wood's rotten."

Jenny ignored him, struggling up a couple of snow-covered steps and beginning to tread warily.

Slowly and cautiously she edged forward until she was directly above her twin.

All she could see were David's head and shoulders and a small section of his chest. Panic filled her as Jenny realised how fast he was sinking. Could she grab him? Would she have the strength to pull him out?

Jenny lay flat and locked her ankles around a post that shifted slightly as she did so.

"I can just reach your hand," she gasped. "Can you stretch up a bit?"

"I can't move – and I don't want to let go." He was shaking all over now.

"Reach up and grab my hand."

"I can't."

"You've got to try. Try now."

With a little yelp of fear David raised a hand, brushed hers and then clamped it back on the joist again.

"That's no good."

"It's all I can do."

"You've got to do better than that," Jenny yelled at him.

"I can't." His voice was dull and stubborn.

"Unless you do, you won't make it. The cold will get you, even if the mud doesn't. Do you understand?" She spoke slowly and ruthlessly.

David tried again, and this time she was just able to grab his hand with both of hers. Jenny pulled as hard as she could, but her brother didn't move an inch. He was just too far down in the mud.

She wrenched at him again and again, exerting every last ounce of strength, but it was no good. David wouldn't come out. What was worse, as he fell back she was sure that he had sunk deeper into the mud.

"What are we going to do?" he asked shakily.

Jenny didn't know, but she had to say something, had to give him hope. "You've got to make more of an effort," she said sternly.

"I can't move!"

"When I grab you again, kick hard."

"That makes me sink deeper."

"It won't!" But Jenny had no idea what was going to happen. All she knew was that she had to reassure her brother, had to give him the will to continue to struggle. "OK," she said, the biting cold in her hands making the circulation horribly painful. "Reach up and kick."

David did his best, and to Jenny's elation their mutual grip was stronger and she felt something give. Could he be coming free?

But he wasn't. Suddenly, David was a dead weight and their hands again parted hopelessly.

Jenny was now sure her only course of action was to cycle back home and call the emergency services. They would surely have some way of getting him out. But could he hang on long enough, or would the mud take him? She felt the agony of indecision. Should she try again? Should she cycle home? Should she –

Then she heard the familiar shrilling of a bicycle bell.

Staggering to her feet, Jenny saw the bike on the track by the creek, shining palely in the moonlight.

"He's back," gasped David in terror. "He's come to finish me off."

"No chance," said Jenny firmly, but she knew they weren't strong enough to fight Bud either separately or together.

"What do you want?" she shouted at the bike.

There was no reaction.

"He's stuck," she shouted. "And I can't get him out."

Still no reaction.

"You've got to help us, Bud. You've got to help."

You can get him out.

"I've tried."

Try again.

"I told you –"

Try again.

Jenny got down on the snow-covered plank again, hooked her feet round the post and told David, "Reach up and kick out."

"I'm too tired."

"Do what I say!"

As he feebly kicked out, David felt a sudden surge of power that filled his body with a warm glow, saturating him with hope and courage and, above all, the will to live.

He kicked out again much more strongly and reached up, this time with both hands, forcing himself to let go.

Jenny also felt the surge of power radiating inside her, suffusing her whole body as she grabbed her twin's hands in hers, pulling with a strength she knew she didn't possess.

David slowly came free with a sucking, gulping sound. He grabbed at a junction of two spars, somehow got a foot on a lower projection and then said, "Let go. Let go of one hand."

Jenny did as she was told, and with the strength of desperation he secured a grip.

"Now the other."

But Jenny was too afraid. She was sure her twin would fall.

"Now the other," he yelled.

Let him go, said Bud's voice in her mind. *Let him go*.

Suddenly Jenny did as she was told and David got another grip just below her. Then, with amazing agility, he began to haul himself up.

Unbelievably, he was now beside her, shivering, covered in mud, but gloriously, wonderfully safe. The bike's bell rang in triumph as David and Jenny lay thankfully on snow and mouldering wood, gasping like stranded fish. Then they slowly stood up, the warm glow draining out of them, facing again the cold dankness of the freezing night.

The bike was stationary, dark and no longer lit by the moon. Jenny and David looked up and saw that a cloud had moved across its surface.

"Thank you, Bud," they both said silently.

The bike stood there for a few seconds and then Bud's thoughts came to both the twins.

I want my dad.

"Mrs Bertram's going to try and contact him tonight."

She's no good.

"She *is* good."

There was a long pause. Then Bud reached David and Jenny again. *Uncle Gilbert's got to die.*

Without waiting for a response, the bike turned,

skidded on the snow and then set off back to Standard Quay in its usual style, just skimming the surface of the snow.

CHAPTER SIXTEEN

"He means that," said David, shivering violently and trying to brush the clinging mud off his clothes. "And if Mrs Bertram doesn't find Bud's father, he'll probably come and get me again."

"He seems to want to get Gilbert Malvin at the moment," replied Jenny miserably. "Hasn't he done enough harm already? Bud doesn't know when to stop."

"He'll never stop," said David flatly. "Not till he's at peace. And he's a long way from that right now."

"He just wants revenge."

"Do you blame him?"

"Revenge isn't a good thing," she snapped.

"You didn't fall into a dry dock!"

Jenny glared at her twin. "So, after all he's done to you, you're sorry for him –"

"In a way. I'm also really scared. But I can still understand. Besides, he saved my life. You know he gave us all his strength. All his will." Jenny sighed. She knew she had Bud to thank for David's life. But she also knew that he was still in great danger. "Mum and Dad are going to be furious.

Look at the state of you. They already think we're behaving like a couple of stupid kids."

"I don't care *how* I look," said David. "Bud saved my life. I thought I was going under – and I would have done. OK, so he chucked me in. But the main thing is that he came back." He paused. "Come on, Jenny – let's go home." David put his arm round her. "You did all you could."

"Did you feel his will?" she asked.

He nodded. "It's amazingly strong. Do you think he was born with it? Or did he put all his heart and soul into it after he died?"

"After he died," Jenny replied slowly. "It's all that's left now, isn't it?"

"Mrs Bertram had better find his dad fast," said David. "If she doesn't I wouldn't like to be Gilbert Malvin, would you? And I wouldn't want to be me, either."

"Maybe he's safe in hospital," she said doubtfully.

"Gilbert Malvin isn't safe anywhere," replied David with conviction.

"I just don't understand it," said Mrs Golding over and over again when the twins shamefacedly re-turned home. "I've never seen you like this before. Is it to do with the snow? A kind of white madness? Thank goodness your dad's still down at the pub." She went upstairs, still complaining, to run a hot bath. "Stay on that mat, David. You look as if you threw yourself in Gatlin Creek. But even you wouldn't be as stupid as that."

David grinned at Jenny through mud-caked lips as their mother disappeared. They had decided to tell her that they had had a snowball fight with Wayne and Dean Martin and that was how they'd got so dirty. Of course they'd have to brief the Martins, but at least the story had prevented their mother asking them too many questions. Anyway, they knew she would never have believed them if they had told her the truth – how they had been involved in a battle of wills with the ghost of a boy on a bike who was able to possess David and make him do exactly as he wanted.

Then the telephone rang.

It was Mrs Bertram. David took the call eagerly, wondering what she had discovered. He could hardly bear to wait as she cross-examined him about what had happened at Gatlin Creek. As he still didn't know what she really believed about Bud, he told her he'd managed to get home "after a bit of bother". Fortunately she didn't enquire about the extent of the bother.

David detected a note of triumph in Mrs Bertram's voice as she quietly told him, "It was much easier than I thought, and it only took a couple of hours."

"You mean – you've found Bud's father?" David

could hardly believe the ease of her discovery. Why hadn't anyone tried before? Then he realised that they hadn't wanted to – that finding Tom Malvin had hardly been a priority.

"I phoned one of Gilbert's oldest friends – not that he's seen him in years. He told me that Tom had been living in Spain for the last thirty years. He married an Englishwoman out there, and as they're both quite old now they had decided to come back."

This is too easy, thought David once again. When things got easy, Bud got restless.

"Where *is* Tom Malvin?"

"Sevenoaks in Kent. They don't sound very well off."

"You mean you've spoken to him?"

"Not yet. I've decided to go and see them. This old friend of Gilbert's is making the arrangements."

"I hope there won't be a delay," said David fervently.

"I'll be going tomorrow, after I've been to see Gilbert in hospital. He's comfortable, by the way – and they say his condition is improving." Despite the good news, Mrs Bertram sounded disapproving, as if David should have asked after Gilbert Malvin first rather than be so concerned about his brother.

"That's great. It's all good news then," he said enthusiastically.

"So far." Mrs Bertram paused. "But there can always be complications," she added darkly and rang off.

CHAPTER SEVENTEEN

David and Jenny hardly slept that night. Jenny kept wondering if Bud would steal into her twin's mind just like 'a thief in the night', which was one of her mother's favourite sayings. She listened carefully, and several times crept out of bed and opened her brother's door, watching him sleeping in the half-light. He seemed peaceful enough.

But David had deliberately feigned sleep when his sister had peered into his bedroom. He knew she wanted to protect him, but he also knew that this was impossible. It was Bud who had protected him, Bud who had developed a last-minute conscience. In one sense, David was glad that the vengeful spirit who so easily possessed him had at last been merciful. Bud was not all bad. Yet, at the same time, he was terrified that he would use him again and this time against Gilbert Malvin. Bud's hatred for his uncle had been strong for a long time. Now David sensed it was nearing fever pitch.

He lay awake, ready to try and repel Bud with his will. But eventually David drifted into uneasy sleep and woke with a terrible start, confusing the ringing of his alarm clock with the all too familiar bicycle bell. He was enormously relieved as he pushed down the button. Had his willpower kept Bud away during the night, or had Bud merely been biding his time? It would be too much to hope that he had gone away for good and the possession was over.

Jenny woke much more fearfully, once again guilty that she had slept. She got up and ran to David's room, not even bothering to knock in her agitation. To her relief when she opened the door Jenny saw her brother sitting up in bed and reading a book.

"You're all right then?" she demanded.

David looked up rather irritably and Jenny saw there were dark patches under his eyes. She guessed he was exhausted.

"Sort of."

"He didn't come?"

"No."

"Did you fight him off?" Jenny asked anxiously.

"No."

"Then —"

"I had a rough night worrying that he *might* come, but he didn't." David gazed fearfully up at Jenny, his bad temper forgotten. "Do you think *every* night's going to be like that?"

"No," she replied firmly. "There's a crisis coming. We've got to be ready for it."

"We? Don't you mean *me*?" David asked bitterly.

"We're in this together. I've got a will too. Bud will have to take us both on," she added fiercely.

David nodded off in maths, and Mrs Rathbone bore down on him angrily, much to the class's delight.

"Leave me alone, Bud," he muttered as she placed a hand on his shoulder.

"I beg your pardon?" Mrs Rathbone was furious.

"I don't want you in my head," David mumbled, and the class hooted with laughter.

"I'm afraid I need to be."

"Get out!" David flailed around, narrowly missing Mrs Rathbone with his fist. He then woke, gazing up at her outraged face in horror. "What are you doing here?" he demanded to renewed laughter.

"I'm here to teach you maths," she thundered. "It's an uphill task if you're asleep in class, David Golding. How about a detention? That should wake you up."

When he finally got home, Jenny was waiting for her twin impatiently. "Trust you to be kept in on an important day like today," she snapped when he told her what had happened.

"I couldn't help it. That Rathbone, she —"

"Don't bother with all that now. Mrs Bertram's

just called. Gilbert Malvin's home. He discharged himself."

"After a heart attack?" David asked in amazement.

"He didn't have one. The doctor says he must have collapsed because of all the stress. But there's something else –"

"Tom Malvin? He's going to come and see Bud?"

"No. That's the problem. He says he parted with Gilbert on the worst possible terms and he doesn't want to rake up the past again. He doesn't want to visit Bud's grave either. Tom Malvin says it'll be too painful." Jenny paused. "Mrs Bertram wasn't likely to tell him that Bud's possessing you, was she?"

"I suppose that would turn him off even more." David looked agitated. Bud hadn't been near him all day but he was sure that he would arrive eventually. Bud seemed to be waiting.

"Mrs Bertram wants us to come to supper anyway," said Jenny. "I spoke to Mum and Dad and they agreed, providing we do our homework first and don't come home late. I think they're pleased we're all going to be good neighbours at last."

"What's the point of going if Tom Malvin's not going to come? Bud will be furious and he'll take it out on me."

"Bud's going to be furious anyway," said Jenny quietly. "And he can take it out on you anywhere. We've got to go. At least we can make some plans."

"There's only one plan that would satisfy Bud." David looked deeply depressed. "The return of his dad."

The Thames was quieter that evening, and as Jenny and David nervously cycled towards Standard Quay the water seemed less sinister as it sluggishly flowed along. The intense cold had also gone, replaced by milder, windless weather that was beginning to melt some of the snow. The going was easier, but as David passed the turn to Gatlin Creek, he shuddered, remembering the horrors of the previous night and Bud's last-minute rescue. He felt curiously light-headed, although David wasn't sure if it was due to Bud's extended absence or his own fatigue. One thing he was sure of was that Bud was going to be angry. Very angry.

When the twins arrived at Standard Quay, they saw Boris, sitting on top of an old car, watching the vicarage intently. As David and Jenny got off their bikes he spat at them, snarled and then jumped down, running towards St James's church.

They watched him pad up the steps and go inside. For a while nothing happened, and then

David shuddered.

"What's the matter?" Jenny asked anxiously.

"Bud touched me. Stroked my mind. Then he was gone." David was trembling. "It was as if he was warning me."

Suddenly Jenny heard the hollow sound of a booming, yet distant, organ. She turned back to the church and saw candlelight flickering at the windows.

"Can you see what I see?" she whispered to David. "Hear what I hear?"

He nodded fearfully and then turned to Standard House for no apparent reason. Jenny's eyes followed her twin's and they watched one of the first-floor windows light up. Now they could both hear the sound of distant, distorted shouting, and Boris ran down the steps of the church, heading towards Standard House.

"Let's get inside the vicarage fast," said Jenny. "Before it all starts happening again."

"Do you think Bud knows his father's not coming?" asked David.

"We haven't got time to find out." Jenny ran up the steps of the vicarage and David followed. As she pounded on the door they could hear the shrill clamour of a bicycle bell. Then the sound of the organ became much louder until it was wheezing in their ears so painfully that they could hardly bear the pressure.

★

When Mrs Bertram had opened the door and they were safely in the dim hall of the vicarage, the twins' ears popped.

"Didn't you hear anything?" gabbled David as she ushered them towards the kitchen.

"Hear anything?" She glanced at him doubtfully. "Hear what?"

But David just shook his head.

When the twins entered the kitchen they discovered Gilbert Malvin sitting in the armchair, looking pale and worn, while Sarah was washing dishes at the sink.

"I'm sorry Tom can't be persuaded to come." Gilbert sounded uneasy. "I only wish I'd contacted him earlier. I never thought he'd return to this country. I'm glad. Very glad." But he was also deeply anxious. "I just hope we can somehow persuade him to come back to Standard Quay some time in the future." Gilbert Malvin paused and then said sadly, "Bud's right to blame me."

"He should blame his father." Mrs Bertram's voice was sharp.

"I don't think we should worry about who's to blame." David was angry. "It's all right for you lot. Bud doesn't get into your head and make you do things you don't want to."

Suddenly, the sound of the bike's bell came from

outside, accompanied by Boris howling.

"Can you hear a bell, Mrs Bertram?" asked David.

She shook her head. "All I can hear is Boris. He's never made that kind of racket before. I can't think what's come over him. He was always such a loving cat, but just recently he's seemed so upset."

"Can *you* hear the bell, Mr Malvin?" David looked at him closely, hoping against hope that at least one of the adults could share his plight.

"I can only hear Boris," he replied.

Outside, the bell shrilled even more loudly and menacingly.

Gilbert Malvin got up and walked stiffly to the window. "Is my Bud out there in the snow?" he muttered to himself as he drew aside the curtain.

Does he believe in the possession at last? wondered Jenny. She remembered how Gilbert had so continually watched the quayside. Had he been hoping to catch a glimpse of Bud all these years?

"I can't see anyone," he said miserably, his eyes searching the snow. "I've never been able to see him, although I always felt him."

Jenny joined him at the window. "Neither can I," she said, trying to be as reassuring as possible, sorry that he didn't have the gift.

The bicycle bell continued to shrill. Then it suddenly stopped and the silence seemed just as loud.

Jenny gazed at her twin and saw Bud in his eyes.

Suddenly David got to his feet with the breadknife in his hand and slowly began to walk towards Gilbert Malvin who had his back to him, still gazing out of the window.

David's eyes were dead and staring ahead. The knife was raised.

Jenny tried to stop David but she couldn't move, despite the fact that she struggled as hard as she could. It was as if she had been frozen by the invisible force of Bud's anger. Then she saw that Mrs Bertram was struggling in a similar way. Were they both going to have to watch Bud make David kill Gilbert Malvin?

Slowly Gilbert turned round. "So it's true," he whispered.

"*You made Dad leave me. Now he'll never come back.*" Bud's voice was harsh and held not the slightest trace of mercy or compassion

Again Jenny tried to force herself to reach David, to grab the knife and take it away, to stop Bud using her brother, turning him into a murderer. He could be locked away for years; the thought was too terrible to contemplate. But the more Jenny tried to move, the more rigid she became.

Gilbert Malvin was trying to reason with Bud now but he sounded weak and ineffective. "I didn't mean to. I'm sorry. I was selfish. He was going to take you, Bud. Take you away from me."

"Put that knife down. *Now*," shouted Mrs Bertram.

Jenny glanced at Sarah who couldn't move either.

"Bud. You've got to leave my brother alone," she yelled. "You can't make him do a terrible thing like this. You can't make David murder him!" But she knew that Bud was determined not to listen to her.

"If you want to kill me, Bud, do it now," said Gilbert Malvin, sounding as if he could no longer bear to negotiate, that he had given up and wanted it all to be over.

"No," wept Mrs Bertram. "We've got so much to live for. Both of us. Let him be. Just let my Gilbert be."

The raised knife was only inches from Gilbert's throat. From David's mouth came the most dreadful snarling, as if all Bud's pent-up loathing was coming together in one infernal sound.

Suddenly, there was an insistent knocking on the front door and then the sound of it being smashed open.

David paused, knife still raised, the snarl still bubbling from his lips, but now he had a puzzled look on his face.

A silence, deep and suffocating, fell across the kitchen as they all gazed at the half-open door. Then a tall man with iron grey hair ran in. His face was long and deeply lined and he was muffled against the unfamiliar English cold in a heavy overcoat and a thick scarf.

David turned, the knife still in his hand.

Jenny watched her twin, wondering if something dreadful was still going to happen.

"*Dad?*"

Tom Malvin looked at David unbelievingly. "Who are you?" he gasped. "I saw you threatening my brother with a knife from outside the window. That's why I forced the door."

"*Don't you know me, Dad?*" Bud's voice trembled.

"It's – it can't be. Why are you imitating my son's voice?" Now Tom Malvin was advancing threateningly on David. "Give the knife to me. Now!"

"He's my brother," shouted Jenny. "He doesn't know what he's doing. But Bud does. His spirit's possessing David. He's nearly killed him – nearly turned him into – "

"Is that you, Bud? Is that really you – in him?" Tom Malvin's eyes were full of tears.

"*I've been waiting for you. Waiting a long time.*"

Tom Malvin opened his arms and the knife dropped from David's hand on to the kitchen floor with a clatter that seemed to go on for a very long time. "I wasn't going to come," Tom muttered. "But something – someone called me. I had to

136

come."

"*It was me, Dad.*" Bud's voice had a sob in it now. "*It was me.*"

"The waiting's over." Tom Malvin still had his arms held open. "Come to me, Bud. Come to me now."

David didn't run towards him, but a shadow seemed to detach itself from around his body. For an instant, Jenny could see the tall, wiry, black-haired boy run towards his father and then disappear again, lost in Tom Malvin's arms.

Soft, gentle snow was falling as, working together, the two brothers uncovered a small headstone in the farthest corner of the graveyard behind the church. Brushing away the snow, Tom Malvin's voice broke time and again as he read out the simple inscription.

BUD MALVIN
DIED DECEMBER 19TH, 1963
REST IN PEACE
BELOVED SON OF THOMAS MALVIN
BELOVED NEPHEW AND GODSON
OF GILBERT MALVIN

"I'm sorry, son," wept Tom. "When you died, something in me died. I couldn't come back. But I'm glad I have now. Forgive me. Please forgive me."

"I never forgot you," said Gilbert sadly. "And I never will."

The Malvin brothers stood there in silence, praying for Bud's spirit.

"I think we should leave Tom and Gilbert together for a while," whispered Mrs Bertram. "They need to be with Bud alone, and after that they've got unfinished business."

"The stolen money?" asked Jenny.

"But didn't Gilbert Malvin give the money back in a different kind of way?" asked David.

"I hope he'll see it that way," said Mrs Bertram miserably. "He'll die if he owns up and has to go to prison."

"I'm sure Tom won't let him do that," replied Jenny.

"They were both wrong," said Mrs Bertram. "Tom for stealing the money, and Gilbert for keeping it. But at least neither of them benefited personally."

As they moved slowly away from the grave, David whispered to Jenny, "I don't think Bud's going to come into my head any more, do you?"

"No," said Jenny decisively. "It's over."

She heard a mewing sound and saw Boris. He padded over and wound himself around her legs. Then the one-eyed tom cat detached himself and seemed to be stalking something. He crouched down, staring intently at a mound of snow, and

gradually the words began to form.
THANKS.
BUD